The P

And The Girl From The

Coffee Shop

by

Terry Towers

The Porn Star And The Girl From The Coffee Shop

Cover by: Terry Towers

Chapter 1

Nadine gave the bag of hot chocolate mix a little jerk, freeing the remaining powder from the bottom of the bag. The powdered mixture poured into the hot chocolate machine, just as she heard the front door of the coffee shop opening, signalling a customer. She groaned inwardly. It was one of those nights where customers trickled in at just the right speed to royally piss her off and hinder her cleaning progress.

After placing the cover back onto the hot chocolate dispenser, she spun around and her heart caught in her throat. Suddenly her annoyance over her nightly routine being disturbed evaporated and her frown turned to a bright smile that reflected in her bright emerald green eyes.

The reason for her change in mood was strutting across the dining room floor towards the front counter, his strides long and confident - bordering on cocky, but not quite. Her eyes scanned him from head to toe, taking note of the scuffed black boots, faded blue jeans and t-shirt stretching across his broad, powerful chest and shoulders. But his most striking feature was his eyes. His deep blue eyes caught hers and a shiver rushed down her spine and a throbbing between her legs commenced - as it did every single time she set eyes on him. Why did his gaze have such an impact on her? She both loved and hated the feeling.

"How's my favourite girl tonight?" he asked as he leaned an elbow on the countertop dividing them and watched as she began to prepare his coffee.

"Same as always, Hunter." She shrugged trying to appear as nonchalant as possible, though she knew she was doing a piss poor job at it. "How was your night?" She looked over at the clock on the cash register; it read 1:00 am. His usual time. What did he do for a living that had him coming in for a coffee this time of night? Her best guess was that he was a bartender, or at least that was the general consensus between the girls working at the coffee shop.

The problem was that the bars didn't close until 2:00 am, so leaving at the peak time for the business seemed unreasonable. He also had an air of confidence about him bordering on arrogance, despite his friendly demeanour. Yeah, he knew how sexy he was, Nadine could see it in is cocky smirk. Normally she had no attraction to men like him, but *dammit* he had *such* an effect on her.

"Wild."

She cocked an eyebrow at him. "That so? Did you just get off work early?" They'd been through the work questions before. She'd ask, and then he'd avoid the question and turn the conversation over to something else.

He nodded. "I did." His smirk widened to a smile as he accepted the coffee she passed him and took a tentative sip.

"So what line of work did you tell me you were in again?" she asked, again attempting to appear nonchalant, and again failing miserably as she accepted the bill he gave her for payment.

"I didn't."

She growled softly as she thrust the bill into the register and counted out his change. As usual he waved it off. Her eyes met his once more. Why she needed to know what he did for a living was beyond her, but it was annoying her to no end that he refused to divulge that information. She knew she had no business asking or getting indignant when he refused to answer, but she was at her wits end with his smug attitude.

Placing a hand on her hip, her eyes narrowed at him. "Are you *ever* going to tell me?"

His jaw clenched and he cocked his head to the side, his eyes moving up and down the length of her causing her to flush and feel highly uncomfortable under his eyes intense scrutiny. "Hmmmm. Dunno."

Pushing back her shyness, she threw her hands up in the air in frustration. "Okay. What do I have to do for you to tell me?"

The soft, sexy smile that sent her heart rate racing touched his lips again, adding to her annoyance. Rubbing his chin as if in contemplation he gave her body one more slow once over. "When is your next night off?"

"Tomorrow night. Why?"

"Go out with me tomorrow night and maybe I'll tell you."

Dumbstruck, Nadine stared at him for a long moment not responding.

Hunter shrugged. "Well, if you don't want to..." Grabbing his coffee he turned to walk away, but she leapt across the counter grabbing his arm.

"No... Wait!"

His smile was gone when he turned back to her, but amusement danced in his eyes. "Change your mind?"

Gotta remain cool, the man already has an ego you can't let him see the affect he has on you, she coached herself. Planting her hands on her hips she took her time moving her eyes up and down his body as he had done to her. When her eyes met his, to her annoyance there wasn't a shred of shyness in his expression, only more amusement. "So I agree and you tell me, correct?"

"Correct."

Upon a moment of hesitation he nodded. "You have yourself a deal. So where do I pick you up?"

Grabbing a pen and a napkin Nadine quickly jotted down her phone number and the address to her tiny one bedroom apartment a few blocks away from the coffee shop. To her dismay her hand shook slightly as she wrote due to her nervousness. *He's just a guy*, she reminded herself. *A fucking hot guy that gets you wet just by looking at you*, a voice in the back of her mind mocked. She ignored that voice as she gave him a bright smile and passed him the napkin with her information on it.

"Well, then I'll be seeing you tomorrow. Eight?"

"Eight," she confirmed. "You gonna give me a hint on where we're going?"

Taking a deep breath in, he exhaled loudly and then shook his head. "Nah. We'll keep it a surprise." With a wink he turned and exited the restaurant.

Nadine watched him leave, flabbergasted at what had just transpired. Despite his slightly cocky demeanour, Nadine had had a crush on him from the first day he'd strolled into the coffee shop. In truth, she suspected his cockiness had a fair amount to do with why she was so smitten with him. They always flirted lightly when he came in, but she never dreamed he'd ask her out. She assumed he had some hot little Barbie look-alike hanging off of his arm when he wasn't in the coffee shop or working at the mysterious occupation.

As Hunter hopped into his Escalade and sped out of the parking lot, a new worry came to the forefront of her mind. How was she going to dress for a date when she had no idea where they were going?

****

For the first time in Hunter's adult life he was nervous about going on a date. The last time he was this nervous he'd been fifteen and he was about to make a move on Becky Tanners, behind the bleachers during a school football game. That was almost twenty years ago. When he put some thought on it, this was the first actual date he'd been on since he began working in the adult industry close to fifteen years ago. Up until that point Hunter Roberts didn't *do* dates.

A good chunk of that nervousness was because he had promised to tell Nadine what he did for a living. Generally, what he did would be something he bragged about. He was a former porn star for God's sake! For years women had been mailing him nude pictures and their worn undergarments hoping for a night with him. Even now as a porn director, producer and photographer he still had a fair amount of women chasing him, though the novelty of those women's attentions had begun to wear on him many years ago.

Pressing the buzzer marked **Nadine Ambers** he waited; going through the ways he could tell her his occupation and have any chance of seeing her again. While his occupation may have brought him an abundance of women out for a single night of fun, establishing a solid, long term relationship with someone special was an entirely different story.

"Hello?"

The soft, sweet sound of Nadine's voice broke into his thoughts. "Hey Nadine? It's Hunter."

Pause.

"K, I'll be right down."

Letting out a loud huff of air, Hunter rocked back on his heels and shoved his hands in his jeans pockets. *Get a handle on yourself Hunter man. It's just a simple date. Not a big deal.* Turning his back to the building he looked out into the parking lot and then off further and watched the traffic zooming past on the adjacent highway. Minutes later the sound of the apartment building's main door opening had him spinning around and he felt as though he'd been slammed in the chest at the sight before him.

At the coffee shop Nadine was a cute girl with her dark hair tied high in a ponytail, and her emerald green eyes giving her an exotic look. And despite the heinous frumpy, brown uniform that they were forced to wear at the coffee shop, he was able to detect her curvy figure. While the majority of the women he had been with over the years were slim to the point that he seriously doubted they ever ate, he preferred women with soft womanly curves - like Nadine's.

"Ummm. Wow." He mentally kicked himself for sounding like such a moron, but the woman standing before him was absolutely stunning. Her long, dark hair cascaded down her back and her eyes sparkled under the overhead light as her eyes slowly worked their way up his body until the met his.

"Wow, huh?" she teased, giving him a wide grin. Running a hand through her hair, she pushed it out of her face and back over her shoulders.

Hunter could feel his face redden at her teasing. Embarrassment; another emotion he never felt often. Clearing his throat he raked a hand through his hair. "Let me try that again. You look absolutely breathtaking Nadine."

Her smile became shy as a blush crept up into her face as she cast her eyes downward, chewing at her bottom lip. An intense, heated silence overtook them for a moment. Finally she glanced back up at him and their eyes locked. "Thank you."

Another silence closed over them. *What is with this nervousness?* He asked himself. Taking a deep breath in and releasing it slowly, he extended his hand to her. "Ready for a fun night?"

Nadine nodded and accepted his outstretched hand. "Yeah, I think so. Can't wait to hear what your mystery job is."

Grasping her hand protectively in his, he led her across the parking lot towards his Escalade. "Maybe I'm unemployed and embarrassed about it," he teased.

She peered over at him and shook her head. "Unemployed and driving an Escalade... Nah, I doubt that."

Hunter laughed. "Why not?"

"Only an idiot would drive a vehicle like that while being unemployed."

"Touché." Unlocking the Escalade he opened the passenger side door for her and helped her in, taking a moment to admire her round ass under her snug fitting black skirt as she turned from him and hopped up.

Being that he was around naked women constantly, it usually took more than a glance at a woman's ass in a skirt to gain his cock's attention. In this instance, however, that's all it took to have his cock rising to attention and straining against the restrictive denim containing it.

****

Nadine was amazed and slightly confused at the change in Hunter's demeanour. He'd never struck her as shy or an easily embarrassed kind of guy, but she'd picked up on both emotions so far tonight. Actually she would almost say that he seemed more nervous than she felt and that was saying a lot!

Regardless, when watching him walk around the front of the truck she couldn't help but feel a stirring between her legs at the sight of him wearing his usual tight blue jeans that hugged his muscular ass and thick thighs. And the tailored, short sleeved black button down shirt made her long to open that shirt and run her hands over the contours of muscle that she knew would be waiting underneath.

Hopping into the SUV behind the steering wheel he slipped the key into the ignition and started the vehicle. Glancing over at her quickly, he gave her a soft smile as he shifted the truck in reverse.

Unable to bite her tongue before the words came out she found herself commenting on his peculiar change in attitude. "So what happened to the cocky, arrogant Hunter?"

She squealed in surprise as the SUV which had been backing up, slammed to a halt and he shifted it into park. Turning in his seat he eyed her a moment, disbelief in his expression. Whether the disbelief was over the fact that someone thought he presented himself as arrogant or that someone had the nerve to call him out on it she was unsure.

"Wait, now..." He cocked a brow up at her as he drummed his fingers along the top of the steering wheel. "You think I'm cocky and arrogant."

Chewing at her lower lip, she gave him a meek shrug. "Yeah, a little."

"Why?"

Oh good God, why did I open my mouth, she groaned inwardly.

"And even more curious. Why would you agree to go out with me tonight if that is how you felt?"

Was he angry? Upset? She couldn't tell, his expression was a blank slate. Taking in a deep breath, she slowly released it. "Because I'm curious about you." She shrugged.

His fingers stopped drumming the steering wheel and his jaw clenched. "Oh, the job thing? You *seriously* came out with me tonight *just* to find out what I did for a living?"

Nice way to start a date Nadine, she chastised herself. But why would he be so testy about it? Unless..."You don't do anything illegal do you?"

His mouth fell open slightly and he snapped it shut quickly and a wide grin spread across his lips, and an amused gleam danced in his eyes. "So let me get this straight. You agreed to a date with someone you think may have been a drug dealer, or hitman or..."

"No... I mean it may have..." She ran a nervous hand through her dark hair and averted her gaze, as she felt the heat rushing to her face.

"So, this crossed your mind and you still agreed to get into a vehicle with me?"

"Well no... I-"

"Do you normally go out with criminals? Would my wearing an orange jumpsuit turn you on? I could find one if you like."

His laughter had her jerking her eyes back up to meet his. Embarrassed at his teasing, she swatted his shoulder. "No. No I would *not* like that. Thanks though." She rolled her eyes at him. "In fact, I *don't* even care anymore what you do."

"You do care!" he challenged.

She gave her head a quick shake, and crossed her arms over her chest. "I don't."

His laughter subsided and his expression turned serious. "Well, let me tell you and then there won't be any more concerns over my line of work."

Nadine put her hand up silencing him before he could tell her. "Like I said... I don't want to know."

"I think you..."

"No." she shook her head, her hair fanning out around her face. "I seriously don't want to know. You can tell me after a few dates."

He clucked his tongue off of the roof of his mouth in consideration and then finally conceded with a nod of his head.

"Alright. Three dates, but if you really want to know I'll tell you now."

Although she was dying to know, especially now, the last thing she wanted was for him to think that her interest in him had anything to so with his occupation. "Deal." Letting out a loud sigh, she tossed a smile at him, relived that *that* very awkward line of conversation was over and they could get on with whatever he had planned for a date.

"Now to get back to the cocky and arrogant comment."

Nadine groaned out loud and a blush coloured her cheeks - yet again.

"Ahhhh, we'll let that pass for now." Giving her a wink he put the SUV back into reverse and they continued backing out of the parking slot.

Closing her eyes, Nadine pinched the bridge of her nose hoping to fend off an impending headache. *Dear God, I hope this gets better.*

Chapter 2

"What is this place?" Nadine asked as she sat up a little straighter in her seat of the SUV so she could get a better look at their surroundings. The conversation had been virtually non-existent for the fifteen minute drive to their destination, up until that point. Each minute of silence increased her nervousness. Shouldn't they be enjoying a steady, light-hearted stream of conversation on a first date? Their conversations and flirtations were always pretty free flowing when at the coffee shop. She feared her mindless comment earlier may have doomed them.

Trying to press her fears to the back of her mind, Nadine's eye scanned the marina as Hunter put the Escalade into park. It was dark, but there were a number of lamps lit lining the marina, giving off a soft and romantic glow. Her eyes followed the lights until they reached the end of the pier. A soft smile touched her lips when her eyes spotted a small table set up with a couple of chairs.

Glancing over at Hunter, he returned her smile and gave her a wink. "Dinner is in the back of the truck." Jumping out of the vehicle, Hunter rushed over to her side of the Escalade and opened her door for her. Taking her hand he helped her down, closing the door behind her.

Keeping her hand firmly in his, he led her to the back of the SUV and pulled out a large picnic basket. When she didn't respond he looked down at her, catching her gaze. "Unless you would prefer..."

"It's perfect," she quickly assured him. Their eyes locked and the awkwardness of the past fifteen minutes during the drive began to slip away, along with her uneasiness.

Satisfied with her response, Hunter led her down to the end of the pier. The atmosphere couldn't have been any more perfect. The warm summer night breeze was perfectly refreshing, without being cold on her bare arms. The moonlight danced over the waves, like shimmering diamonds, as they rolled in with a low tranquil roar.

It. Was. Breathtaking.

Setting the picnic basket on the small, two person table, he proceeded to pull her seat out for her.

"So do you do this for all your dates?" Nadine teased as she sat down and watched

Hunter unload the picnic basket. "Nah. You'd be the guinea pig for this particular type of date."

His eyes caught hers once again and a shiver rushed down her spine. While their time in the Escalade had been slightly awkward, it seemed to have been forgotten now and the familiar yearning for him was once more ignited within her. His eyes dipped from her eyes to her cleavage that peeked from behind the red sleeveless blouse. When his eyes returned to meet hers again, the fire and hunger was once again within them.

She swiped her tongue along her lower lip, yearning to feel his lips brushing against hers. How many times over the past few months had she fantasized about feeling his lips on hers? Countless times. Sure, he was cocky with a hint of arrogance, but she supposed that was part of what made him so damned sexy. She had no doubt that a night with him would be nothing short of incredible.

"Nadine?"

The sound of her name released her from her thoughts and she jerked her eyes up to meet his, flushing yet again. "I'm sorry I was..." She ran a shaky hand through her silken hair. "Sorry."

"Wine?" He nodded towards the two bottles in his hands. Red in the left hand, white in the right.

She looked from one bottle to the other. Normally not much of a drinker, she'd never tasted wine that she could remember before so she was clueless as to which to choose.

"White please," she responded, taking a chance, choosing strictly based on the appeal of the bottle.

"White it is." With the finesse of a skilled bartender Hunter opened the bottle, popping the cock.

Hmmm, maybe he is a bartender. The timetable of when he showed up at the coffee shop didn't really jive with the job of a bartender, but it *was* possible. It would explain the cockiness. Considering how good he looked he was sure to be hit on by dozens of women each night, surely that would bolster the ego. Realizing where her thoughts were headed, she gave her head a quick shake and returned her focus back on Hunter. *No sense in wondering about it now Nadine, the deal was three dates.*

She watched Hunter finish unloading the large wicker picnic basket, complete with candles that he lit and settled at the center of the table. A soft, sultry melody began playing that enhanced the magic of the evening.

"Wow, you are really going all out tonight."

He nodded as he filled two glasses of wine. "Not what you'd expect from someone so cocky and arrogant huh?"

Nadine huffed making Hunter grin.

"That was such a stupid thing for me to say. I'm sorry. I was just nervous."

Passing her a glass of wine, he gave her a curious look as he took a seat across from her. "Why on earth would you be nervous? You're never nervous when I go into the coffee shop, why now?"

Taking a long swig from her wine to settle her nerves she swallowed the cool liquid down with a grimace. White wine was definitely on her 'never drink again' list. Glancing up at Hunter she could see the amused twinkle in his eyes, but he didn't say anything. He simply waited for her to answer his question.

"Well, at the coffee shop the counter is like a buffer between us and the customers."

"A buffer?" he raised a brow at her and took a sip from his wine. "How's that?"

"See, you're like any old customer that comes in when at work. We chat, I flirt to get my tip and you leave."

"Whoa, wait. So those sweet little smiles and whatnot when I came in was all for the tip!" he feigned outrage, though the amusement still gleamed in his gorgeous blue eyes. "All men get that kind of treatment!"

Nadine rolled her eyes at his dramatics and took another swig of the vile tasting wine. "Yes. *But*. With you I mean it."

A burst of laughter erupted from Hunter, so suddenly that he accidently tipped over his wine glass, drenching his brown three-quarter length jacket. "Ah shit!" he exclaimed, while still laughing.

Oh damn! Jumping up from her chair she rushed over to him. Grabbing a napkin from the picnic basket she began to wipe at the wine, not even realizing that she was coming dangerously close to his groin.

"Whoa! Wait!" Hunter grabbed her wrist just as she was about to wipe the front of his pants.

Nadine's mouth dropped open as she realized what she was about to do. How many times was she going to embarrass herself tonight? She snapped her mouth shut and covered her face with her hand, giving her head a little shake unable to look him in the eye.

"You know what... I think I know how to fix this. So we can relax and have a fun evening."

With her hand still covering her face she spread her index and middle finger and peeked up at him through her fingers. "More wine?" A soft, nervous laugh escaped her.

Slipping his hand from her wrist he entwined his fingers with hers. Removing her hand from her face, he placed it on his chest and then slipped his arm around her waist and pulled her close.

Nadine's breath caught in her throat as her body pressed against his. The deep, woodsy scent of his cologne begged her to get closer. She lifted her eyes to meet his and the amusement that had just been in his eyes had turned to a look that was hungry and feral.

Oh God! She sighed softly. Her hand on his chest, flattened and she traced the lines of hard muscle under the cotton button down shirt he was wearing. There was no doubt in her mind what was about to happen and she wanted it. She wanted it badly.

"Still nervous?" he asked, his voice low and deep, making her stomach flutter.

Her first instinct was to lie and deny it, but she didn't. "A little."

He took a deep breath in and released it slowly. Releasing her hand he touched her cheek, and then traced her lower lip with his thumb. Her heart rate accelerated and the temptation to suck his thumb into her mouth was near impossible to deny, but she pushed the instinct back.

Her hands moved up his chest to his shoulders, and she pressed herself tighter against him. The length and hardness of his erection pressed against her stomach through their layers of clothing, taking her by surprise and spiking the desire building within her.

Hunter removed his thumb from her lips and slipped his hand to the back of her head as he inched his face closer to hers. With their gazes locked, his mouth ended its decent an inch from hers and paused there. Their breaths intermingled and breathing synchronized.

"Still nervous," he whispered.

"Very," she admitted, her body trembling against his. She fisted his shirt under his jacket, attempting to calm herself. A dull ache ignited between her legs, and she could feel her juices beginning to moisten her panties in anticipation. *Just kiss him Nadine*, she coached herself.

He waited a moment longer. The tension between them was becoming so thick it could be cut with a knife. Nadine thought she was going to die from the anticipation. Just when she thought she couldn't take another moment of this sweet torture he closed the final inch between their lips.

Nadine moaned softly as his lips brushed against hers. She longed to let herself go, but struggled to keep herself reined in. Hunter nipped at her lower lip, and she moaned a second time, pressing herself tighter to him, subconsciously grinding her pelvis against the hard ridge of his cock.

Hunter released her lip and brushed his lips against hers a second time. "Still nervous?" he chuckled softly as his lips brushed up and down the side of her neck sending an intense shiver through her.

"Terrified," she admitted softly, closing her eyes and tilting her head to the side allowing his lips better access to the sensitive flesh. She'd never wanted anyone so badly and never had anyone make her feel so vulnerable with a simple kiss.

Hunter's string of kisses ran across her collarbone, towards her lips once more. "You're so good you could do this for a living," she teased, although her tone reflected the tension within her.

"Maybe I do," Hunter replied softly.

She would have laughed at how insane his comment was, but his lips were on hers again and this time with an intense hunger and need.

****

Hunter couldn't have restrained himself another moment if he had wanted to - which he didn't. Her hair smelt of sweet apple, drawing him in. And her soft, moist lips were begging him to kiss them. His lips claimed hers with a need he'd never felt in a long, long time - if ever.

He had no idea if it was just the anticipation, or the fact that it had been years since he'd felt such an intense, genuine attraction for a woman, but he needed her. She moaned once more against his lips and he immediately deepened the kiss, his tongue thrusting past her lips to duel with hers.

With each sigh and soft moan that came from her, his cock would jerk in excitement. Over the years sex had become a job and lost much of the appeal it had when he was young. But with Nadine, his need and excitement was renewed. It felt so good it was indescribable.

Hunter slid his hand up the back of her sleeveless blouse and felt the soft, creamy flesh underneath. Oh, how he longed to touch and explore more of her. Pulling his mouth from hers, he trailed kisses back along her jawline to her ear.

Nadine sighed softly in his ear. Her sigh was so sensual and erotic his body tensed against her as he fought to keep his cock under control. Both his dick and his balls were becoming painfully hard, but he loved every second of it.

"Still nervous?" he couldn't help himself but tease - whispering in her ear.

"No," she gasped, "all I can think about is how much I want you."

He stopped his string of kisses and nips down her neck to pull back and look her in the eye. The desire burning within her eyes was a reflection of his own need. A part of him was demanding he lift her up onto the small table, hike up her skirt and slam his cock deep into her. He could only imagine how warm and tight she'd be around his massive length. Whether she would allow things to progress that far he didn't know and doubted, but he was craving to try.

The other part of him knew there was something special about the woman pressing against him. She was bringing about feelings he hadn't felt in a long time and so he wanted to savour the feelings of need and anticipation.

"Oh, you have no idea who much I want you Nadine. It's taking every ounce of willpower to restrain myself." He prayed she wouldn't press him. If she did he'd never be able to deny her.

She reached up and touched his cheek and then traced his jawline with her index finger. "Me too."

He bent and brushed his lips across hers again. "And that's why we're going to sit back down, get to know each other better and enjoy the evening." His resolve waivered when he noticed the disappointment shining in her eyes, but he held strong. "Then I'm going to drop you home and kick myself until the next time we go out that I didn't take the opportunity to go further with you right now."

She caught her lower lip between her teeth and a tiny smile touched her lips. "The next time?"

"I hope so."

"Me too."

Chapter 3

"A kiss? That's it," Samantha huffed, accompanied with a roll of her eyes.

Not all of us date men only for a fast fuck Sam, Nadine longed to retort, but kept the quip to herself, not wanting to provoke her co-worker. Samantha had had her eye on Hunter for some time now, but Hunter never seemed to pay much attention, so she'd lost interest. If provoked, however, Samantha might decide to double her efforts on him. Something Nadine *did not* want.

"Well, I think he was quite a gentleman. And, it was one *hell* of a kiss."

Samantha shrugged and was about to turn away from Nadine to go back to her station at the drive-thru window when her eyes spotted Hunter. "Well speak of the devil."

Nadine, with her back to the front entrance of the coffee shop turned to see Hunter strutting across the dining room floor, heading straight for her. Her heart rate accelerated and her pussy clenched at the mere sight of him. He looked as sexy - no, sexier - than ever, because this time she didn't have to fantasize about how his body would feel against hers. Now she knew.

She made her way to the front counter cursing the ugly uniform, hairnet and shit brown visor she was required to wear. She wanted to look good for him, and the uniform wasn't doing her any favours, in her mind.

At the counter he motioned for her to lean over the brown marble counter towards him. Frowning, she did as requested, leaning forward.

"Is the boss working?" he asked leaning into her and speaking just loud enough for only her to hear.

"No, it's just me, Sam and Jenny tonight."

"Good."

Before she could reply, he captured her chin in his hand and tilted her face upwards as he lowered his mouth to hers. Shocked she simply rolled with it, welcoming his warm lips and demanding tongue. For the moment she completely forgot where she was or who was working with her and she became lost in him.

To her disappointment the kiss ended far quicker than she would have liked.

"Your co-worker was giving us a look. Figured I'd give her something to stare at."

She felt her cheeks grow warm as she looked over her right shoulder at Samantha, who was indeed staring at them with open hostility. Why Samantha refused to be happy for the other girls at the coffee shop Nadine couldn't figure out. Not to long ago Samantha had tried everything she could think of to ruin their co-worker Alyssa's relationship with one of the firefighters across the street. Nadine prayed she and Hunter weren't next on Samantha's hit list.

Where Samantha Larson was concerned no woman's boyfriend, fiancé or husband was safe.

"You do realize that will only provoke her," Nadine whispered to him before setting to work on preparing his coffee, without needing to ask him what he wanted.

Hunter shrugged and gave her a sheepish grin, not bothering to give Samantha another look. "Don't worry about her."

Easy for you to say, she grumbled to herself, but returned his smile. His heart was in the right place and his dropping in was easily the highlight of her day thus far. The majority of her morning and afternoon had been spent replaying the night with him in her head - every exquisite moment. At twenty-six, she was feeling like a teenager with a crush again.

It occurred to her that Hunter was dropping by much earlier than he usually did. "So what's up with the early night?"

"Things wrapped up early." He leaned over and rested his elbows on the counter. "Which is why I'm here." Nadine passed him the coffee without charging him, which he accepted and took a tentative sip and nodded his approval. "Perfect."

Giving him a condescending smirk, Nadine rolled her eyes at him. "Isn't it *always*."

"Touché. So what's the chance of you getting out of here?"

"I'm off at two."

"Yeah, but that's five hours away." He frowned, giving her a wounded look, pleading to her with his eyes.

Laughing Nadine shook her head. "I don't-"

"Nadine. I need to speak with you out back for a moment," the voice of her other co-worker, Jenny, cut into her refusal. Jenny was the no-nonsense overnight worker. Most of the girls that worked there saw her as cool enough to be a friend, but wise enough to be a parental figure.

"One sec." Nadine raised her finger to Hunter and he nodded his compliance. With a quick look over at Samantha who was still watching her and Hunter, but with a little less interest than before, she rushed into the kitchen to see what Jenny needed.

Entering the kitchen she was presented with Jenny holding her purse in one hand and her jacket in the other. "Go on girl. Get going."

"I can't just leave you with Samantha," Nadine protested, but was already removing her visor and pulling the hairnet from her hair as she said it. Jenny wasn't the type to take no for an answer, so while she felt the need to object she knew she'd never win the battle of wills with the older woman.

"Look. I can't remember the last time you've come into work with that giddy, school girl crush look on your face. It's about time." Once Nadine unclipped her headset from her belt, Jenny helped her into her jacket.

"But... I'm wearing my uniform and smell like coffee. I can't go out-"

"Then make him take you home to change," Jenny interrupted, giving her a nudge out of the kitchen and towards the front of the store.

"Samantha is going to freak," Nadine protested further keeping her voice low so only Jenny could hear her as they cleared the kitchen and emerged behind the counter of the coffee shop.

"I'll take care of her," Jenny assured her, not bothering to be discreet in her answer.

Nadine's next attempt to protest was cut short when she caught sight of Samantha leaning over the counter and attempting to chat with a disinterested, yet polite, Hunter. Deciding to stake her claim then and there, Nadine made her way around the counter to Hunter and wrapped her arm around his waist, pressing herself tight to his side.

"Looks like I can get off early after all," she announced to Hunter, but her eyes were glued to Samantha's. Knowing she had Samantha's full attention she turned back to him and ran her fingertip along his collarbone. "But you'll have to take me home a minute, so I can get out of these clothes."

Clearly amused, a wide grin spread across his face as he looked from one woman to the other. "Whatever you want, *sweetheart*."

Saying a couple of quick goodbyes to Jenny and Sam, Nadine and Hunter left the coffee shop hand-in-hand. Nadine could feel Sam's eyes shooting daggers at her back and took a slight satisfaction in the feeling. *I'm going to have to remember to thank Jenny at the bachelorette party tomorrow night.*

****

"I go to the coffee shop because I love coffee, so why would I be offended by the smell of it?" Hunter stated as he and Nadine entered her small, one bedroom apartment several blocks away from the coffee shop.

"Gee, and I thought you came to the coffee shop for me," Nadine teased, shrugging off her jacket and slinging it over the back of the kitchen chair.

Slipping his arm around her waist he pulled he tight and kissed her soundly, sending her pulse racing. "You're a bonus."

Groaning, she wiggled her way out of his embrace. "I gotta shower. Give me fifteen minutes. The offensive coffee odour may not offend you, but it does me."

"Maybe I find the smell of coffee sexy." Hunter reached for her a second time and with a laugh Nadine ducked out of his reach. With an exasperated sigh Hunter threw his hands up in the air in surrender and proceeded to remove his leather jacket, tossing it on top of Nadine's. "Alright. Fine. You win. Go get your shower."

****

Hunter flipped mindlessly through the television channels as he waited for Nadine to shower. Just thinking of her in the next room naked with water cascading down her curvaceous body was driving him insane. He'd never wanted to masturbate so badly in his damned life as he did now.

True to her word, ten minutes from stepping into the shower he heard the water being turned off. If she exited the bathroom barefoot and in just a towel he wasn't sure if he'd be able to control himself. There was only so much a man could reasonably take and he'd used up a good chunk of his restraint the previous night.

They hadn't planned on seeing each other again for a few days, but the draw to her made it impossible for him to stay away. He'd been in the porn business for so long that directing porn barely aroused him anymore. Tonight, however, he'd been hard for the majority of the shoot. Not because of the actors, but because the scene he was shooting kept reminding him of Nadine and how much he wanted her, so when the shoot ended early, he took it as a sign to see her.

Hunter's head turned quickly towards the bathroom door when he heard it opening. A burst of steam escaped the room first followed by Nadine wrapped in a pink puffy towel. She was barefoot and her long dark hair wrapped up turban style in a matching pink towel.

Oh, you have got to be kidding me, he groaned to himself at the sight of her. His cock jerked violently in his pants and he shifted his position on the sofa attempting to ease some of the distress in his pants.

"Sorry I forgot to bring a change of clothing with me." She gave him a shrug and a tiny smile as she proceeded to walk - her hips swaying seductively - past him to disappear into the bedroom and close the door behind her.

****

She doubted Hunter believed her little story about forgetting a change of clothing. In truth, she wasn't sure what she had wanted to come out of her little seduction attempt. The way he looked at her, his eyes following her every step, made her tremble inside. She'd been tossing around the idea of giving herself to him tonight. It had been so long since she'd had a man, she barely remembered what it was like anymore. But on the other hand she *was* still getting to know him.

She pulled the towel wrapped around her hair and brushed her hair out and then dropped the towel that was wrapped around her body. Naked, she made her way over to her closet and flung open the door, examining the contents. Sexy? Casual? Chic? She had no idea what to wear.

Despite her contempt for her co-worker Samantha, she did admire how Sam set her sights on a man and had no qualms about taking what she wanted. She grabbed for a pair of jeans from the top shelf, but then her eyes caught sight of a never worn before red satin teddy. It fell to her knees and had delicate spaghetti straps. With a shake of her head she continued to look, deciding that it was simply too early for that now.

Opting for a pair of red plaid boxers and a t-shirt she pulled her dark hair up into a pony tail. Giving her reflection another inspection in the full length mirror hooked onto the backside of her bedroom door she shrugged. *If this goes anywhere he's going to see me like this one day anyhow, right?*

Taking a deep breath in she grabbed the door handle and pulled the door open to see Hunter aimlessly flipping through the channels on the television. Upon seeing her, he immediately flicked off the television and patted the empty spot beside him on the sofa.

"From the look of your outfit I'm assuming we're staying here."

Oh shit, he wanted to go out? Groaning inwardly she kicked herself for not asking before she got dressed. "I can go change. I just thought-"

Hunter chuckled. "I'm teasing. You look beautiful. T-shirts and boxers look extremely sexy on women." He nodded towards the spot next to him and gave it another pat. "Come sit with me."

Sitting down beside him she cuddled close, and was immediately enclosed within his strong embrace, her back to his front.

"So you still think I'm... Hmmm.... How did you say it, cocky and arrogant?"

She made an attempt to wiggle out of his embrace to face him, but he held her tight, swept her hair away from one side of her neck and placed a soft kiss there. Nadine's body melted into him. "My first impression may have been a little harsh," she replied laughing lightly. Her laugher suddenly turned to a sigh as his lips touched her neck a second time, and began to trail a line of kisses up her neck from her collarbone to her ear lobe.

Hunter pulled her tighter against him, his rapidly thickening cock pressing against her ass. "So what do you think now?"

The fire between her legs ignited and she moaned softly. She had no idea what she thought. Her mind was rapidly giving way to the reactions her body was having due to his closeness and the sweet woodsy scent of his cologne. "I think..." Her breath caught in her throat as he slipped a hand up under her t-shirt to cup her breast in his hand, over the pink lace bra she was wearing.

He was so distracting. "I think..." Reaching behind her to slip her hand behind his neck, she stretched out on the sofa spreading her legs slightly to relieve some of the building tension. "I want you Hunter."

He growled softly behind her and she looked up to peer into his hungry stormy blue eyes. "I think we need to talk Nadine," he said softly, his voice strained with the tension that mirrored her own.

Nadine shook her head and stretched up further, pulling his lips down to hers. "Later." She couldn't have concentrated on a conversation if she'd tried. He hesitated a moment as if he was deciding whether he should insist or not. Suddenly, he claimed her lips - roughly dominating her lips with his own. As their lips and tongues frolicked and teased his fingers pinched her hardening nipple. Nadine cried out against his mouth and ground her ass against his rock hard cock between their clothing.

Oh, how she wanted his cock and needed relief from her building tension. While his hand on her breast slipped to the other and proceeded to roll her nipple between his fingers, his other hand slid down her stomach and under the waistband of her boxers to her shaven pussy.

Squirming over him, Nadine spread her legs wider welcoming his exploring hand and fingers. Nadine rubbed back against him with more force, frustrated over the layers of clothing separating their bodies.

Her teasing caused Hunter to tear his mouth from hers as he groaned loudly and cupped her mound in his hand. He slipped two fingers between her wet folds and ran then the length of her slit, lingering at her swollen clit to pinch it softly.

"So wet, Nadine. You're driving me mad," Hunter whispered into her ear.

His soft, seductive voice flowed through her and Nadine bucked wildly at his hand. Hunter refused to let up; he stroked her a second and third time, with each run of his fingers she grew closer to her climax.

Desperate to feel him, she reached behind her and stroked the ridge of his cock over his jeans. His body tensed under her and he breathed in sharply. "Oh Nadine..." As he spoke he spread her pussy lips wide and thrust two fingers into her needy pussy. The sudden invasion of his fingers as they stroked her inner wall was all she needed. She cried out and her body trembled as she was overtaken by the rush of her climax.

Once the aftershocks wore off, she quickly turned in his arms and slipped to her knees on the floor between his legs. She needed to touch him, taste him and return to him the pleasure he'd just given to her.

Chapter 4

Hunter knew he needed to stop her and explain to her his career and make her understand what it meant for them. The problem was that the sight of her between his legs looking up at him with her large, stunning eyes as she undid his jeans was more stimulation than he could stand.

"Oh Nadine, I-" His thoughts and last ditch attempt to explain himself was cut off when she unzipped his jeans and pulled his aching cock from under his boxer briefs.

"My God you're *big* Hunter," she sighed as she began to stroke him in firm fluid motions.

Words were now lost on him entirely as he watched her, his hands clenching at his sides. It was taking every last ounce of energy for him to keep from slipping his hands to the back of her head and urge her lips down onto the lip of his cock.

Pre-cum began to seep from the tip and slide down the length of his shaft and over her hand. She moaned softly and then licked up the trail of his cum until her lips circled around the head of his shaft. Closing his eyes, he let his head drop back against the back of the sofa indulging in the feel of her warm, soft mouth taking him in.

Her tongue swirled around the head of his cock, periodically flicking at the slit. Her mouth enclosed over the head once more and unable to hold himself back any longer he opened his eyes up, grasped her head in his hands and gently urged her mouth down further on his length.

Needing to see her beautiful body as she took him in, he leaned forward, grabbed the hem of her shirt and tugged it upwards. Reluctantly she released his cock, to lift her hands over her head and he pulled the t-shirt all the way off and tossed it to the floor beside her. Reaching behind herself, Nadine unclasped her bra and peeled it off her shoulders and tossed it to join her shirt.

Nadine was about to lean back down when he stopped her. "Take off the boxers." He needed to see all of her. Taking her lower lip between her teeth she stepped back a foot from him, hooked her thumbs into the waistband of her boxers and tugged them down, letting them drop to her feet and stepping out of them.

"My God, your stunning Nadine," his voice was barely more than a whisper as his eyes roamed up and down her body. Her breasts, with large dark nipples were plump. Her figure was a nice curvy hourglass with a nice round bottom that he would love to spank as he fucked her from behind. He groaned inwardly as he realized his thoughts were getting away from him.

Slow and easy Hunter, slow and easy, he coached himself. But then his eyes settled on her shaven pussy and the thoughts began to get away on him once again. Once his eyes finished their wandering of her shapely body, he glanced back down at his dick, which was leaking once more with his cum.

Her eyes followed his eyes and she immediately took his cue. Dropping back down to her knees in front of him, she went back to work on his dick, diligently sucking him while using her hand to cover the remaining inches, her hand moving in time with her mouth. The sensations flowing through him were more intense than he could remember them ever being. His stomach was in knots as he attempted to hold himself back.

"God you look good sucking me baby," he managed to groan out. Her soft moan sending soft vibrations through him was her only response.

While she continued the delicious torture of his dick she used her free hand to pull down on his jeans until she had them down around his knees. She immediately grasped his balls in her free hand and squeezed lightly.

Hunter groaned loudly and began to thrust up into her mouth. Up and down her head bobbed on his dick, driving him to near insanity. He was longing to let go, but his pride forced him to hold back. He could normally go for hours, under the right circumstances and if he paced himself. But with her he was ready to blow his load already. It was highly embarrassing.

Just when he thought he couldn't stand another second she changed her technique running her tongue down the length of shaft and then back up to the tip again. She ran her tongue down the opposite side, and this time her head dipped lower taking one of his balls into her mouth, sucking lightly, while kneading the other with her hand. Dropping his first ball from her mouth with a light plopping sound she took in the other.

Unable to contain himself any longer he took his cock in his hand and began to stroke himself fast and hard. His whole body became tense; he was seconds away. His cock throbbed and just as he was about to come, Nadine released his ball from her mouth, batted his hand from his cock and quickly took over sucking him, while stroking the base. Within seconds of taking him into her mouth, he groaned loudly as his cock exploded, with a violent stream of his cum slamming against the back of her mouth.

As his heart rate slowed he watched as she finished swallowing his cum and then let his depleted shaft slip from her lips. Wiping a drop of cum from her chin with her index finger she slipped her finger into her mouth sucking off his cum.

"Damn Nadine!"

****

Before she even knew what was happening, Hunter had lifted her up and laid her down on her back on the sofa. He then stood and stripped off his clothing revealing his finely toned body to her. Her whole body quivered in anticipation as he sank back down onto the sofa, stretching out over her, bracing his weight with a hand at the side of her head.

"You're gorgeous," she gasped as she fingered the fine muscle of his chest. The muscle rippled under her touch, arousing her further. Nadine's eyes peered up into his and the intensity of his hunger still flamed within them.

He smiled down at her and gave her a quick wink. "Don't be giving me too many compliments honey, I might get cocky," he teased, brushing his lips across hers.

Laughing, she rolled her eyes at him. "I think I'm beginning to really like cocky." She teased back as she slipped a hand to the back of his neck and pulled his mouth down tighter to hers.

"Glad to hear it." He pressed his body a little tighter to hers. His cock which was already beginning to thicken, slipped between her drenched and dripping pussy lips.

"Please!" She wiggled and bucked under him, anxious to feel his long, thick shaft stretching her.

"Not yet honey," he whispered in her ear before nipping at her lobe. The warmth of his breath sent a shiver through her and the throbbing between her legs commenced.

She groaned inwardly. Why was he being so cruel? She both loved and hated his restraint. "Hunter..."

His mouth moved lower, trailing a string of kisses across her collarbone and then down her chest to claim her first nipple. His tongue circled and flicked her nipple into a tight bud. She cried out as he nipped lightly at her nipple, and slipped his hand between her legs, cupping her mound.

"Your breasts are perfect," he murmured as his mouth moved from the first to the second repeating the process on the second one causing her to whimper and squirm under him.

Once the second nipple was rock solid, he continued his mouth's exploration of her body, working his way down with a line of butterfly kisses. With each inch his mouth came closer to her dripping wet pussy, the more intense her anguish to have him slamming into her became.

By the time his mouth reached her mound she was a mess. She slipped her hands into his unruly hair and urged his mouth down lower until his breath tickled her pussy.

Hunter slid a finger between her folds from her anus to her clit and then spread her pussy lips wide, exposing her fully to him. A sliver of shyness crept into her as he watched him between her legs, hunger in his eyes as he teased her pussy and clit. The shyness quickly turned to desire when he ran his tongue along her slit.

"Oh God Hunter. Please!" she bucked against his mouth as he licked the length of her a second time.

"*Damn* you taste good," he groaned, licking her a third time and then flicking her clit with his tongue. A shot a hot desire rushed through her, leaving her light-headed. Her whole body was becoming tense, her heart racing. It was good. *Too* good.

Hunter licked her yet again, then slipped one of her legs over his shoulder, spreading her wider and thrusting his tongue into her heated core. She cried out fisting his hair and bucking against his mouth as he began to tongue fuck her.

"I need you in me," she groaned. His tongue was so good, and his fingers stroking her clit was driving her near insanity. She'd never been with someone so skilled in her life. Every touch, every lick, and every stroke of his fingers and tongue brought her closer to her point of no return.

"Come for me baby," he murmured and then buried his face between her legs once more.

She doubted she'd seen anything more erotic as seeing him between her legs, his tongue alternating between working her clit and then thrusting into her. Wave upon wave of pleasure washed over her, until she reached her breaking point. "Oh God Hunter, I'm coming." she cried out as a final, intense rush of pleasure ran through her from her head to explode between her legs. A rush of her juices greeted his tongue and he eagerly lapped up her nectar.

She trembled as she came down from her high, panting rapidly.

"So fucking good," Hunter mumbled as he ran his tongue along her a final time before sitting up and then repositioning himself to lie alongside her on the sofa, pulling her tight against him.

With a sigh, Nadine cuddled tight to him, laying her head on his chest and draping a leg across his. "I've never had anyone so... *amazingly* good before!"

He chuckled and when she picked her head up to peer up at him she noticed a faint glimmer of a blush touching his cheeks. "Not sure I would say I was amazingly good, but thanks." He squeezed her tighter and kissed the top of her head.

"Hmmm. Oh, you are," she assured him placing her head back down on his chest and tracing the hard muscle in his chest and shoulders. "I'm so glad you stopped by tonight."

"Me too honey. Me too."

****

"Since Alex didn't like the idea of us getting strippers, I picked up some videos for us." Bride-to-be, Jade, waved several DVD's above her head as she made her way across the living room towards the player.

"Oh God. Porn Jade? Seriously?" Nadine laughed, and found herself slightly uncomfortable with the idea of watching porn with a group of her co-workers, but if that's what Jade wanted... It was all in good fun, right?

"So, how did it go with Hunter last night?" Jennie asked as she sat down beside Nadine on the floral print loveseat and passed her a cocktail.

Nadine grinned. "Amazing."

Nadine's mind raced back to her night with Hunter. She'd never wanted to fuck someone so badly in her life, but he'd denied her. However, she certainly couldn't complain about the foreplay or how skilled he was in the oral department. She'd fallen to sleep, naked in his arms and awoke to breakfast cooking with him wearing nothing but her apron and that sweet sexy smile of his.

A part of her was actually glad they hadn't had sex. It gave her something to anticipate and look forward to. Their next date was tomorrow night and he was going to reveal the big secret about his occupation. He'd offered to simply tell her a number of times, several times insisting, but she refused. She was actually having a bit of fun trying to figure it out on her own. The only thing she could figure was that he was a bartender. It was the only thing that made sense to her. He had the looks, the charisma and attitude that she'd expect. That had to be it.

"So ladies!" At the sound of Jade's voice all twelve women attending the bachelorette party turned their heads, ending their respective conversations and focused their attention on the bride-to-be. "This first video is called... *The Pussy Bandit,"* she announced slipping the disc in the player and pressing the start button on the remote.

Laughing at the absurdity of the title, Nadine glanced over at Jenny and rolled her eyes.

"When do you see him again," Jenny asked as they waited for the movie to start.

"Tomorrow night." Nadine's attention was distracted as a woman walked onto the screen, and into the set's kitchen, dressed as a 1970's suburban housewife - floral print sundress and apron, over her extra large breasts, and slender waist.

The woman on the screen turned and gasped as a tall, lean man wearing a black mask covering the upper part of his face entered the scene. "What are you doing here!" The woman onscreen exclaimed!"

"I'm here for your sweet pussy," the man in the mask replied.

Nadine was in the process of bringing her drink to her lips when she froze, the glass two inches from her mouth. That voice was familiar... *Too* familiar. She examined the man on screen a little closer. His jaw was chiselled and dark hair unruly - just like Hunter. He approached the woman, grabbed her hips and spun her around, bending her over the kitchen table.

"My husband will be home soon," the woman on screen proclaimed.

"Don't worry, we have enough time," the robber responded pulling her skirt up and then hooking his thumbs in the waistband of her thong and yanking them down exposing her pussy to him and to the audience.

Nadine watched the robber undo his black pants and then continued to watch as the scene unfolded, becoming more and more aware that she knew the 'robber' with each minute that passed. *Nah, it can't be him.* Twenty minutes of sex went on, the actors repositioning themselves several times. The scene completed with the woman on her knees in front of him waiting for him to spray her face with his cum.

With a loud groan that churned Nadine's stomach the 'robber' spewed his cum on her. Once he was finished unloading she wiped her face, grinning foolishly up at him. "Please, at least show me your face. I'll never tell a soul," she assured him as she rose to her feet and slowly peeled his mask from his eyes.

Nadine thought she was going to be sick as the robber was revealed to be none other than Hunter. *Her* Hunter. A couple of her co-workers gasped also recognizing him.

"Oh-my-God! Isn't that..." One of her co-workers said.

"That's Nadine's new boyfriend," Samantha squealed with obvious delight.

Nadine whipped her head around to glare at the grinning Samantha.

"Well, it's true isn't it?" Samantha asked taking a sip from her beer. "So is he *really* that good of a fuck Nadine?"

Nadine ran a shaky hand through her hair and shook her head. "I-I don't-"

"Zip it Samantha," Jenny snapped standing and rushing over to the player and ejecting the disc. "I think we've seen enough."

"I want to see the case." It had to be a mistake. Someone who looked like him. She'd heard a number of times that everyone had a twin somewhere in the world. Maybe that was Hunter's?

Jenny carried the movie over and passed it to her. Flipping the case over, she looked at the screen shots. None showed the actor without his mask. Looking to the bottom of the case to the credits she noticed the actors name was **Hunter Longcock**. Different last name, but the same first name. How tacky. Nadine swallowed back the hurt that was bubbling up within her. She needed to see him. Was *this* the mysterious job? No wonder he kept it a secret. It had to be a mistake. Maybe a dumb thing he did to make money while in college? She needed to know.

"I gotta go," she murmured standing and tossing the video onto the coffee table in front of her in disgust.

The room fell silent, all eyes on her as she made her way towards the front door, grabbing her jacket off of the back of a kitchen chair as she walked by.

"Where are you going hun?" Jenny asked coming up behind her.

"To Hunter's house." Nadine pulled on her jacket as she reached for the door handle.

"Do you think that's wise? Maybe you need some time..."

"No. I need to know what this is all about."

"Want me to come with you hun?"

Turning back to face Jenny she gave the older woman an appreciative smile. "I'll be okay. I just need to talk to him."

"Alright." Giving her a quick hug, Jenny stepped back. "Call me if you need me."

With a nod Nadine turned her back to the bachelorette party and left.

Chapter 5

Hunter was in the process of lowering himself into a warm aromatherapy bath, a secret indulgence that he'd have never admitted to anyone, when he heard the doorbell. The temptation to ignore it was great, but the person on the other side seemed insistent pressing the buzzer rapidly and insistently.

"Coming, coming," Hunter grumbled more to himself then to the person on the other side of the door, securing a towel around his waist as he made his way to the front door. Grabbing the doorknob, he yanked open the door to see Nadine standing before him.

A smile touched his lips as her looked down at her, but it quickly faded as he noticed the grim look on her face. "Wow, Nadine. Come on in. I thought you were attending a bachelorette party tonight?" Stepping aside, he ushered her into his lavish five bedroom house on the outskirts of Portland.

"I was." She walked past him, avoiding his eyes.

"So what happened? Not to say I'm not excited to see you. I'm... thrilled honestly."

She eyes surveyed the foyer as she shrugged off her jacket. "I left. They started watching porn and it made me think of you." She was dressed casually, in jeans and a t-shirt. As usual she looked as sexy as hell.

Hunter's body froze, with Nadine's jacket in hand. There was no way that of all the porn in the world the women in at the bachelorette party would have seen one of his was there? There was thousands upon thousands of videos out there, roughly two dozen of which he acted in, and they were created over ten years ago. He'd *directed* hundreds of videos, but all of which were directed under a different name in the off chance he decided to switch careers.

He cleared the lump that was beginning to form in his throat, as he opened the coat closet and hung up her black three quarter length jacket. "Why did it remind you of me?"

She spun around to face him and for the first time since she'd entered the house, looked him in the eye. "Are you going to deny it was you?"

This wasn't the way he'd wanted her to find out. He had a whole night planned for her tomorrow night, which was her night off, where he was going to tell her the fill truth about his current and previous career. Taking a deep breath in, he let it out slowly trying to gather his thoughts.

"Come on into the living room and sit down, while I grab a pair of boxers and we'll talk." He reached out and touched her cheek, and to his relief she didn't jerk away. "Okay?"

She nodded and allowed herself to be ushered into the living room, which was elegant in design with high cathedral ceilings, and a lit fireplace with marble mantle at the back. Once she was seated on the cream coloured leather sofa he rushed off for the bedroom, thankful for the few extra minute to figure out a way to make what he had to say sound good enough that she wouldn't leave tonight and never come back.

****

For the past twenty minutes, the length of time it took to drive to Hunter's place from Jade's, Nadine's mind couldn't keep from going back to the image of Hunter of the television fucking that big breasted, blonde woman. She wondered how many videos was he in. How many women had he been with? Was he still doing porn? Could she accept it if he was? She just didn't know. Sure, all men had pasts, but anyone that wanted to could see *her* man fucking random women whenever they wanted. It actually made her sick to her stomach thinking about it.

"Penny for your thoughts?"

Pulled from her thoughts Nadine glanced up at Hunter to see he had removed the towel and pulled on a pair of black fleece lounge pants, sitting low on his hips. He hadn't bothered with a shirt, leaving his muscular chest bare. If she hadn't been so upset over her discovery, her body would have been on fire with need for him. Especially after last night. However, the confusion she was feeling was overriding everything else, at the moment.

"What do you do for a living Hunter?" Nadine asked and then held her breath awaiting the answer.

With a sigh, Hunter sat down beside her on the sofa and took her hand. She relaxed slightly as their fingers entwined.

"Okay, I have no idea what video you saw-"

"*The Pussy Bandid.*" she offered.

"Wow. Okay." Hunter ran a hand through his unruly hair. "Yeah, that was one of mine."

"Oh God," she groaned. A part of her was hoping he'd deny it and that it had been some huge mistake. As much as she didn't want to ask, she needed to know. "How many are you in? Are you still making them? Is that the career that you've been hiding?"

"Well, no. I'm no longer an actor."

Oh, thank God! Her spirits lifted. The past was the past right?

"But I'm still making them."

Her spirits fell as quickly as they were rose. "But... you just said..." She tried to read his expression, as if she could find out all she needed to know simply looking at him, but all she saw was concern in his eyes.

"I'm a pornographic producer and director."

"So you're a pornographer?" She had no idea how she felt over that additional information. Maybe he wasn't fucking on film anymore, but he spent his days watching others fucking. All those slender, big breasted, beautiful women with blonde hair and stunning tans... Jealousy surged through her and she tried to press it down.

"I promise you Nadine, it's not what you expect it to be."

"So you don't watch people fuck all evening, every evening?"

Hunter sighed. "It's a job Nadine. That's all."

"Do you get aroused?"

"It's not quite like that. I've been in the business a long time..."

"How long?"

Hunter clucked his tongue off of the roof of his mouth. "About fifteen years. Five years as an actor and ten as a producer and director."

Fifteen years in the fucking business? My God!

"Believe it or not, when you're exposed to it constantly sex loses much of the appeal."

"So is that why you didn't want to... You're just not-"

Hunter's face blanched and he shook his head, taking both of her hands in his. "Oh no Nadine. You're the first woman in a long, long time that I'm dying to be with. You have no idea how much restraint it took last night to just hold you."

"But why didn't you?" Her mind was racing. Why her when he could have his choice of sexy women, with big boob and tiny waists? Those women would know each and every way to pleasure a man, when her knowledge was limited in comparison. It made no sense.

"Because I wanted you know this about me first. What I do."

Nadine chewed at her lower lip. "I just... I don't get how you *can't* be attracted to the women in your movies."

Keeping her hands in his, he gave them a reassuring squeeze. His jaw clenched, but his expression became unreadable. A silence overtook the room as Nadine waited for Hunter to respond. With every second lapsed, she became more concerned she'd angered him with her pressing.

Finally he nodded, a smile touching his lips. "I have an idea."

Cocking her head to the side she regarded him with curiosity. "What kind of idea?"

"You're off tomorrow and I have an afternoon shoot. I changed the time so we go could out tomorrow night. Come with me." His smile widened and she noticed an exuberance entering his eyes.

Nadine shook her head. "Oh, *hell* no Hunter." She attempted to pull her hands from him, but he refused to release them.

Hunter shrugged. "Why not?"

"Well... I..." There were dozens of reason why not, but at the same time she couldn't deny that she was intrigued. What went on at a shoot? Maybe he was being honest and it was just work and nothing more than that to him. It would certainly be interesting to see for herself. "It would be awkward Hunter. People having sex and me..." she crinkled up her nose at him. "And me... *watching*?"

"The actors won't care. Why not?"

Nadine opened her mouth to give him another reason why not, but snapped it shut again. The idea was seriously perking her interest. "A porn shoot. Seriously?"

Hunter shrugged again and gave her a wicked wink. "It'll be fun. I promise."

With a loud sigh she returned his smile. "Alright. I'll go." *Maybe it will be fun*, she told herself, her excitement over the idea rising.

When he attempted to lean in to kiss her, she raised a hand and flattened her palm against his chest. "But..."

Hunter froze waiting for her to continue.

"I can't guarantee I'll be okay with this. You have to promise to respect my feelings on this. Cause if I can't deal with the porn then..." The last thing she wanted was to stop spending time with him, there was something growing between them, something she'd never felt before. But at the same time she knew he'd never stop what he did for a living, by the looks of his home it was evident it made a very comfortable living for him, so she'd never ask him to.

His smile faded as he nodded. "I promise."

The worry in his expression tore at her heart. She had no doubt that his feelings for her was at par with what she was feeling from him. It was shocking to her that such an attachment could develop so quickly; a few months of flirting at the coffee shop and a few evenings together. But it was.

With the issue of his occupation settled - for now - the fact that he was sitting before her in just a pair of bottoms came rushing to the forefront of her mind. To her dismay her eyes glanced down his body and paused at her groin as her desire for him ignited.

"Not tonight honey."

Nadine's face flushed at being caught and her eyes quickly jumped back to meet his. "I don't know what you're talking about," she defended herself laughing.

Sitting back on the sofa, Hunter pulled her back against him - her back to his front and wrapped her arms around her. Nadine couldn't have stopped the sigh that escaped her lips as she settled into his strong embrace if she tried.

Hunter brushed her hair away from her neck and softly caressed the skin of her neck with his lips. "How about we just talk. And then if all goes well tomorrow..." He nipped at her earlobe and sent a rush down her spine.

"Not the best way to convince me to behave myself Hunter," she moaned, closing her eyes and laying her head against his shoulder.

Chuckling he kissed her temple as he pulled her tighter against him. "Hmmm. perhaps not. Maybe I just can't help myself."

Nadine smiled, keeping her eyes closed and enjoying the warmth of his breath on her neck that was sending pleasurable shivers through her. *Hmmm, that makes two of us.*

Chapter 6

Hunter had no clue whether bringing Nadine onto the set was a good or bad idea. He hoped that when she saw how professional the shootings were she'd realize that for him it was what it was - a job. Nothing more or less.

"This way." Keeping her hand firmly held in his, Hunter led the visibly nervous Nadine through the mansion he'd rented for the week in order to film the movie, and towards the pool in the back. The scene was to take place at the pool.

"So what is the movie about?" she asked as they approached the glass double doors leading to the massive pool area where the crew and actors were already ready for them.

Hunter chuckled. "A rich housewife gets bored of her billionaire husband and decides to have some fun with the Latino pool boy."

Nadine threw back her head and laughed, her dark eyes twinkling with amusement as she looked up at him. "Serious?"

"As a heart attack."

Nadine groaned. "Isn't that a little cliché."

"But it sells." Hunter gave her a wink before opening the glass door for her. Stepping aside he allowed her to enter before him.

"I'm a bit nervous," she admitted quietly as she brushed past him, through the threshold.

"Why, you planning on performing on camera today?" he teased, reclaiming her hand and proceeding to led her to the set.

Rolling her eyes, she jabbed in him the ribs with her elbow. "No. But I've never watched people have sex before."

"Well, I'm glad you get to share this first with me."

*****

She wasn't sure what she'd expected, but the scene before her wasn't it. The pool area was lavish and simply spectacular. She had a hard time believing that people actually lived there. At one end of the massive, oval pool was a waterfall. The droplets of water shone like diamonds under the sunlight. There was a hot tub that could easily fit a dozen people at the other end.

One either side of the pool were lines of lounge chairs and ten foot tall hedges surrounding the pool area, keeping what was going on there private from would-be prying eyes.

"This is *really* beautiful."

"Yeah, it is." Hunter gave her hand a tug and guided her towards an attractive couple sitting at the edge of the pool, their feet dangling in the water. "You can meet the talent."

Hearing them approaching, the two actors got to their feet.

"Nadine. Let me introduce the stars of the show - Mark Sanchez and Celine Gunner."

Nadine eyed both of them as she shook their hands, not sure how to take them. While they were good looking from afar, they were stunning up close. Mark was tall, lean Latino man that Nadine doubted would be a day over twenty-two. The woman was nearly as tall, slender, big breasts and appeared to be in her late twenties.

"So this is the Nadine from the coffee shop?" Celine asked, giving Hunter a teasing smile.

"You know, he used to go out of his way to drop by the coffee shop every night you were working," Mark added.

Celine started to laugh as Hunter ran a nervous hand through his hair and shifted his weight from foot to foot like a nervous teenager. "He even gave one of the girls twenty bucks to keep him informed on your days off."

Nadine's eyes jumped back to Hunter who was starting to flush slightly. She was tempted to join in the teasing, but refrained. She wasn't sure how to take his bribing her co-workers for her schedule. It was both flattering and kind of creepy. However, she'd been learning that Hunter was slightly arrogant and aggressive about getting what he wanted which was actually part of his charm. It was certainly a "Hunter" thing to do.

Hunter cleared his throat and met Nadine's gaze for a moment. "Yeah, well. Enough talk. Let's get to work." Grabbing her hand again, Hunter tugged her away from the two porn stars and towards a couple of director chairs. "People, we're starting in ten. Get set up and ready to shoot."

"You paid off Jenny didn't ya?"

Frowning, Hunter looked down at her and shook his head. "No. How could you believe I'd do such a thing?"

"Hunter..."

Hunter let out a chuckle. "She did it for free."

Nadine laughed. It figured. Jenny loved playing Cupid.

*****

Hunter was thankful that his actors were pros because he couldn't focus on the scene between Mark and Celine no matter how much he tried. His entire focus was on Nadine. She'd been hesitant to watch - at first - but now she seemed almost intrigued at the action going on before them. Celine was currently on her knees in front of Mark, licking and sucking his cock as though it was the last lollipop on earth.

"How could you *not* get aroused by this," she finally whispered over to him.

"Like I told you. It's work. After a while you get used to it," he whispered back.

To his surprise Nadine slipped her hand over his lap to cup his groin. Hunter inhaled sharply and his cock immediately began to thicken, under her touch. Hunter looked around them - no one was paying any attention to them, all eyes were on the stars.

"Ummmm. Nadine," He glanced down nervously to see her looking up at him, a mischievous gleam in her eyes.

She chewed at her lower lip and smiled. "Just checking."

Nadine gave his shaft a squeeze and Hunter attempted to push down the desire flaming within him. "For the record, I wasn't hard until you provoked me."

"I know. But still... It's so..." She squirmed in her seat making him ache to slip his hand down the front of her jeans and feel the wet heat between her legs.

"So, are you okay with this?" Hunter held his breath, waiting for her answer.

In response, Nadine stroked the ridge of his cock a little harder and he had to bite down on his tongue to keep from groaning his pleasure.

"Nadine, we're working," he managed to chock out, both wanting her to stop and aching for her to become more aggressive with her teasing.

Giving him a wide grin she removed her hand and settled it on his upper thigh. "How much longer left in the scene?"

"We're just doing one scene today and I think we have as much coverage as we need." Turning his attention back to the couple they watched for a moment as Celine continued her tongue's exploration of the actor's cock. "Okay. We have enough oral footage. Celine, switch to your back and masturbate yourself while Mark jacks off on you pussy. Then it's a wrap for the day.

****

Nadine was amazed at how professional Hunter could make a sex shoot. To his word, he didn't seem aroused at what was going on around them, but focused on getting the best possible footage. The entire crew seemed engrossed in their specific job, unfazed by the fact that what they were shooting was sex.

She supposed they were all accustomed to being in this type of atmosphere. She on the other hand, was sitting in her chair uncomfortably with panties soaked in her juices and she yearned to try some of what she'd been watching on the gorgeous man sitting beside her.

She turned from Hunter's strong, chiselled profile, back to the actors. The woman groaned, loud and dramatically as she came. As planned, Mark gave his cock another couple long and hard jerks and then shot his load over Celine's pussy and stomach, in several powerful spurts.

Nadine's pussy clenched as she envisioned the couple to be her and Hunter. Turning her head to look at Hunter she caught his gaze and for the first time since they'd arrived on set she saw the desire raging within his blue eyes. She was tempted to inch her hand up higher to rub his erect dick through his jeans again, but held herself back. The crew was beginning to turn off their equipment and put it away.

"So where are we heading once you're finished?"

"It's a surprise." Hunter gave her a wink and stood as he approached the actors who were cleaning up, spoke with them and then the crew. Twenty minutes later the cast and crew had left the mansion leaving just them alone. Looking at her watch she found herself shocked to realize that close to six hours had gone by. For one sex scene! It really *was* work.

Rising from her chair, she made her way over to Hunter who was looking out into the pool, a look of contemplation on his face. The day had given way to night and the moonlight reflected in the pool. The shimmering moonlight in combination to the sound of the pool waterfall added tranquility and romance to the atmosphere.

"Are we done for the day," she asked as she stepped up behind him and wrapped her arms around his waist, leaning her forehead against his back.

"Well, the work part," Hunter confirmed, turning in her arms so he was embracing her, pulling her tight against him. "So, what did you think?"

Sliding her hands up his chest and around his neck, she pressed herself against him. "As long as you're no longer acting in them, I think I can handle it."

She felt the tension within him, slowly deplete as he lowered his mouth to hers, kissing her softly. "So, what do you think about spending the night here?"

She looked around them and back at the massive mansion to her back. It looked more like an Arabian place than a house. "Really?"

Never being in a place so beautiful or exotic, she couldn't wait to explore the house.

"Uh-huh."

Excitement gleamed in her eyes and a huge smile spread across her lips as she turned back to face him. "I'd love it!"

"Then let me give you a tour," pulling away from her, he kept her hand held protectively within his as they started off on the tour.

*****

"And this is the master bedroom," Hunter announced as he opened the door to reveal a massive bedroom, which was the last stop on their tour.

Excitement gleamed in her eyes as Nadine walked past him and to the center of the room. Hoping that she would be fine with his career once she was there for a scene, he'd prepared the room for them. A massive oval, marble hot tub was running and waiting, with chilled champagne sitting at the side. Rose petals had been sprinkled on the king sized bed, with a large bouquet of red roses sitting on the center. The lighting was dimmed to a warm honey glow and a soft, romantic melody played in the background, just loud enough to hear, but not be intrusive.

"Wow, when did you do all this," she asked as she snatched the roses from the bed and brought them up to her nose, inhaling deeply. "All this wasn't necessary."

Hunter grinned as he walked over to her, "Perhaps I overshot a little."

Nadine set the roses back on the bed, and stepped into his arms. "It's perfect."

A wave of relief washed over Hunter as he pulled her closer and lowered his mouth to hers. The feelings of insecurity with a woman were foreign to him. However, with Nadine they were there, as if he needed to strive to be a better man for her, when just a few weeks ago that thought would never have come to his mind. To his surprise he liked the feelings because they were pushing him unlike he'd been pushed before.

Fisting the front of his shirt Nadine led him towards the hot tub. With each step they got closer to the tub, the harder his cock became pressing against his jeans, and aching to be released. While he'd planned and hoped that tonight would be the night, he had no intention of pushing it. But as they stopped, Nadine spun back around to face him, took a couple more steps backwards so he had a full view of her body and began to strip.

Slowly, meticulously, she began to undo the buttons to her blouse. Not being able to restrain himself, Hunter took a step towards her, but was halted in his tracks as she pressed a palm to his chest and pushed him back, giving him a silent shake of her head.

"Nadine..." Despite his protest, a grin touched his lips.

She continued unbuttoning her pink blouse to reveal a black lace bra underneath. Shrugging off the blouse she tossed it to the floor at his feet and began working the button and zip on her jeans. Spinning around so that her back was to him, she bent over and she tugged the jeans down over her hips, revealing a pair of black lace boy shorts that accented the roundness of her ass.

His cock jerked, screaming to be freed. *Do I undress? Do I wait for her?* He was conflicted, not wanting to ruin the seduction she had planned.

Still bent over, Nadine glanced over her shoulder and caught his gaze. The fire he was feeling reflected in her emerald eyes. With a soft whoosh sound her jeans fell to the floor at her feet. Straightening up, she stepped out of the jeans and kicked them to the side, as she slowly turned to face him.

"You planning on getting in the hot tub fully clothed?" She asked as she reached behind her and unclasped her bra.

Laughing and feeling slightly embarrassed, he began to frantically undress for her, while keeping his eyes glued on her. She let the straps of her bra slide from her shoulders and down her arms, slowly letting the bra fall to display for him her stunning breasts. Her large dark nipples began to tighten with the sudden cool air caressing them. His clothing was shed without the finesse of Nadine's stripping for him and he was fully naked just as she was hooking her thumbs into the waistband of her panties.

"No, allow me." Dropping to his knees, he grabbed her waist, pulled her close to him and began to place butterfly kisses down her torso. Nadine's body shivered as his mouth reached the waistband of her panties. He looked up and caught her gaze as he peeled her panties down her hips, exposing her shaven pussy to him. With another jerk the panties fell to the floor and he tossed them aside once she stepped out of them.

"Oh God Hunter," she moaned, spreading her legs a little wider as he pulled her closer and placed a kiss on her pelvis. Hunter's body was so on edge and his balls so tight that he was scared he might explode if he didn't calm himself.

"I've been wanting to taste you all day," he murmured as he swept two fingers between her soft, wet folds and then sucked her juices from his fingers. She was so wet, and needy for him, it was driving him wild.

"Hold onto my shoulders," he instructed and she did as told, as he spread her pussy lips wide and buried his face between her legs, lapping up the juices that had been pooling between her legs.

She clutched tight to his shoulders and cried out as his tongue circled and then flicked her clit. Her warm juices, teased his tongue as he ran it along the full length of slit again. Her body trembled over him, and her soft whimpers were like sweet erotic music to his ears and urged him to continue on until he felt the rush of her climax as it greeted his tongue.

Once she was licked dry, he thrust his tongue deep into her. He tongue fucked her needy pussy until she was bucking against his mouth and her fingernails dug so deep into his shoulders she was leaving deep crescent indents in his muscled skin.

"I. Can. Barely stand, Hunter," she moaned, her legs trembling under her.

"I'll catch you baby," he murmured in response, though his words were muffled and he doubted she'd even heard him. He gripped tight to her hips in case her legs gave out so he could catch her as he doubled his efforts, eager to taste her sweet release.

"Gonna come!" she cried out, bucking wildly against his mouth.

Hunter began stroking her clit, to add to the sensations rushing through her. It worked. Her whimpers became louder, and more frequent. There was no way they were going to make it to the hot tub once she came; the thought came to his mind just as she screamed out his name one final time, her pussy clenched around his tongue and a rush of her nectar greeted his probing tongue and mouth.

As predicted, seconds after her release her knees buckled under her weight. As promised he caught her, and gently laid her down onto the soft white shag rug under them. She was murmuring his name, her eyes glazed over from the power of her desire and orgasm.

As he stretched out beside her, he took a moment to admire her stunning breasts which were jiggling with each deep inward breath. She closed her eyes and when she opened them back up the raging desire was still there, taunting him.

He had to have her. *Now!*

Chapter 7

"Damn, Nadine!" Hunter whispered as he leaned over her kissing her violently.

Nadine surrendered to his demanding lips and tongue, aroused by the taste of her cum on him. Slipping an arm around his waist she tugged his hard, beautiful body onto hers, while spreading her legs to accommodate him.

All she'd been able to think about while watching the porn actors all afternoon was him and how good it was going to feel to finally have him in her. The day long wait had been sheer agony, but now he was touching her, kissing her and settling himself between her thighs.

His massive cock, which she guessed to be roughly eleven inches pressed against her opening making her pussy ache for it. His lips kissed their way down her neck and across her collarbone quickly making their way to her first breast.

"God, Hunter. I want you in me!" She slipped her hand between their bodies and wrapped her fingers around his shaft. He groaned, his body stiffening above her as his tongue lashed out and flicked her already hard nipple.

"Not yet." His tongue finishing its torment of her first nipple moved across to her other nipple. He nipped at her second nipple sending a sharp jolt of pleasure and pain through her. She cried out, her back arching seeking more. Firming her grip on his cock, she began to stroke his length in fast and fluid motions.

"Nadine..." he groaned, swirling his tongue around her nipple and nipping a second time.

Nadine slipped his cock, which was dripping with his pre-cum between her pussy lips. She bucked against his cock, pressing the head against the entrance to her core. Releasing her nipple from between his teeth, he looked up and into her eyes, with a feral hunger that she'd never seen in the eyes of any man and without a single word; he slammed himself fast, hard and deep into her.

"Holy fuck, you feel good," he groaned, his voice breaking as he spoke.

She cried out her pleasure as his long thick length filled and stretched her so completely that she thought she was going to be ripped in two. He groaned loudly, his body tense as he kept himself embedded deep within her. Letting out a slow ragged breath, Nadine attempted to control the waves of pleasure flowing through her. But while she attempted to control her body's response to his cock's invasion and slow down the waves flowing through her, she still wanted more.

She'd just gotten her breathing slowed when Hunter pulled out and slammed into her a second time. Her fingernails dug into his back and she bucked against him. Giving up on holding back she moved under him, urging him to move fast and harder.

Taking the hint, Hunter began to slam into her at a frantic pace, the head of his dick stroking her g-spot with each inward thrust. His cock slammed repeatedly into her wet pussy, taking her to the brink. Wrapping her legs around his waist, she pulled him into her as he thrust downward, tilting her pelvis to pull him in as deeply as possible.

"I need to come," she gasped.

Hunter lifted his head from her shoulder to look her in the eye. The intensity in his stare was all she needed. With a moan of satisfaction, Nadine's legs tightened around his waist and a rush of relief and pleasure flowed over her as her pussy tightened around his cock and she hit her climax. The rush of her warm nectar coated his dick as she came in a series of orgasms that left her physically drained, but completely sated.

"Oh fuck, come over my cock honey," Hunter growled in her ear. "So damned good."

"Oh yes!" Good, didn't even begin to describe how he felt within her.

"Ride me while I come."

Before Nadine was able to respond, Hunter had flipped onto his back and rolled her onto him. However, being so wrapped up in the moment, neither one of them considered how close they were to the lip of the hot tub and before she realized what was happening Nadine felt her knee slipped into the tub. With a squeal, she grabbed onto his arms for balance, but instead pulled him into the tub with her. Their bodies tumbled into the tub, creating a giant splash that soaked the floor around the tub.

Wiping the water from her face, she felt laughter bubbling up within her. Opening her eyes, she locked gazes with Hunter's which contained a mixture of emotions: lust, amusement, confusion. Not being able to stop it, laughter erupted from within her. At the sound of her laughing, Hunter's bemused expression changed and he joined her laughing as he grabbed her around the waist and pulled her onto his lap so she was straddling him.

*****

Smooth Hunter, real smooth, Hunter chided himself as his laughter subsided and the needs of his dick took over. Again, he found himself amazed at how 'out of sorts' she made him feel. Sliding a hand behind her head, his thumb stroked her cheek as his eyes wandered the length of her body. Her body gleamed with water as droplets slid down her breasts and stomach.

His cock and balls were both aching. His need was too intense; he needed to bury himself deep within her and end his suffering. "Take me in and ride me honey," he managed to choke out, as he pulled her mouth down to his.

As their tongues duelled, she sat sank down onto his cock, encasing his shaft in her moist warmth. He groaned against her mouth as he grabbed onto her hips and began to guide her, up and down on his length as he thrust up into her.

While he wanted to continue the feelings rushing through him and was thoroughly enjoying the sight of her as she pulled her mouth from his, arched her back and began to ride him in earnest, he couldn't control the impending ejaculation if he'd tried.

She rode him, hard and fast, punishing his eager cock with her demanding pussy. The sight of her bucking against him was too erotic. The sounds she was making were too sexy and the feel of her tight pussy surrounding him was too deliciously good.

"Fuck, Nadine. I'm coming," he groaned as he pulled her down tight to him, meeting her partway with each thrust. Water splashed over the side of the tub, further soaking the floor around it.

"Oh yes! Yes! Yes! Yes!" she panted in response, as she began to rotate her hips in a circular motion as she moved up and down on him.

His cock throbbed and balls tightened to a near unbearable brink, preparing for release. "Come with me," he coached as he thrust up in her a final time.

With a load feral groan, Hunter pulled her tight onto him slamming as deep as possible into her welcoming pussy and release. A surge of cum shot from his cock, releasing all the pent up tension that had accumulated within him all day, in one pleasure filled moment. She gyrated on him for another moment and then her body jerked - almost violently - over him, she cried out his name and a gush of her warm juices joined his in her channel.

"My God, you feel *amazing* Nadine. So tight. So perfect."

At the sound of his voice, she straightened up on him and opened her dark eyes to catch his gaze and give him a coy grin. "Ummmm. Maybe it isn't that I'm tight, but you're just *huge*."

He could feel his face grow warm at her comment. Since when was he shy, or easily embarrassed over his cock? He groaned inwardly. Normally he'd have a cocky reply for a comment like that. But he was coming up empty.

So much for being cocky, he mused.

Nadine let her body fall against his, and she lazily kissed her way up his neck, sending pleasurable shivers through him. "Penny for your thoughts," she whispered in his ear, seconds before nipping lightly at his ear lobe.

"I was wondering if you still think I'm arrogant and cocky," he teased, kissing her temple.

Nadine laughed softly as she began to kiss her way across his jaw until she brushed her lips across his. "Very cocky and arrogant, but I've grown to love those qualities about you."

"Hmmm. Glad to hear I've grown on you."

She pulled back slightly so their eyes met. The affection was so evident within those stunning dark eyes that it scared him slightly. She was falling for him - hard and fast.

A part of him was scared of the prospect; he'd made it a point all his life to avoid such emotional connections. Get off and get out, had been his motto. But the other part relished having such a pure, sweet, amazing woman caring for him. It was at that moment that he realized, he was ready to settle down and he was anxious to see where things led with the beauty looking down at him with such intense affection.

Another thought occurred to him as they gazed into each others eyes. They'd been so wrapped up in each other he'd forgotten to use one of the condoms he'd left in the bedside table. That was a slip of mind that *never* happened to him. *Ever.* Being in his line of business safe sex was always his number one priority. The sweet girl from the coffee shop had an incredible hold on him, and it was a scary sort of good.

*****

"You're still going to continue dating him!" Samantha shook her head at Nadine. "Do you have any idea the stuff he did in that video? Not for the feint of heart I'll say that much."

"You all watched it after I left!" Anger filled Nadine as she looked at Samantha and the guilty faces of a couple of other co-workers. The thought of all her female co-workers seeing Hunter fucking random women appalled her. Sure, she'd decided to accept his occupation, and the fact that there were videos floating around, but it hadn't occurred to her that everyone she knew would be watching said videos. Jenny had the night off, so she was there to fight this battle alone. Fortunately, she had just gotten off and was waiting for Hunter to pick her up. She was shocked Jenny would have allowed them to continue playing it.

"He's your boyfriend, not ours," Samantha defended giving Nadine a smirk. "Was curious on what he was into. We weren't going to let it ruin our fun." The other two coffee shop girls gasped at Samantha's words and immediately scampered off, leaving Samantha and Nadine alone.

"That is rude even for you Sam."

Samantha spread her hands out, palms up. "Hey, any of the girls could have taken it out at any time."

Samantha opened for mouth to respond when the sound of a ding chimed in their headsets, indicating it was time for Sam to get back to work. With a smug smile, she turned on her heel and made her way to the drive-thru section to take the customers order.

Pulling off her headset, Nadine angrily tossed it onto the back counter. *She's really a piece of work*, she growled to herself as her other two co-workers emerged from the hiding spot in the back kitchen. She was about to confront the other two when Hunter came strolling into the coffee shop, looking as sexy as ever.

"Hey honey, you rea-" his sentence was cut off and an uneasy smile touched his lips as he glanced at her two co-workers whose faces had turned red while adverting their gazes. Quickly regaining his composure, he raised an inquiring brow at Nadine.

"Yeah, let me grab my jacket." She rushed to the kitchen and grabbed her jacket and purse from the staff coat rack. Pulling her jacket on as she walked, she made her way back to Hunter who appeared to now be unfazed by her co-workers reactions to him and was chatting lightly with them.

Hoping to get him out of the coffee shop before Samantha was finished with her customer; she rushed to his side, grabbed his hand and gave it a tug. "Ready. Let's go."

She knew she shouldn't let Samantha rile her up, or make her feel uncomfortable about what Hunter did for a living - or used to do. But she'd had enough confrontation for one day and even though she hated having to ask him, she felt she needed to know exactly what was on those videos so Samantha couldn't railroad her again. She had no doubt Samantha would be renting the entire Hunter collection now that Sam knew she could use the videos against her.

Once they were out of the coffee shop, Hunter stopped dead in his tracks nearly pulling her from her feet in the process. "So what was that all about anyhow?"

*****

"Alright. You're out of your uniform and into comfortable clothes. We're at my place. We have champagne, not wine. Not a soul around. Tell me what was going on at the coffee shop." Hunter settled down beside her on the leather sofa, while passing her a glass of champagne.

She'd refused to talk about the coffee shop awkwardness, but now that they were home he was determined to get to the bottom of it. When he'd dropped her off at work that afternoon after spending the night and morning with her she couldn't have been happier. He saw a gleam in her eyes that he loved. But that gleam was gone for some reason throughout the day and anxiety had replaced it.

"The girls watched the video after I left," Nadine blurted after taking a deep sip from her glass.

Awwww damn. That hadn't even occurred to him. In truth, it didn't matter all that much to him, which he supposed was why he hadn't thought much about it. But, he could see why it would bother Nadine.

"And Samantha said there was some nasty stuff on that video..." She finished off the glass of champagne and then refilled her glass, refusing to meet his eyes.

Well, shit fuck. He raked his brain trying to remember what was on that video. He'd done so many movies, and the kinks and intensity varied greatly between videos.

"I wish I could tell you what they saw, but I honestly don't remember what was on that one. I've done so many..." Her body tensed next to him and he immediately cursed himself so stating it like that.

"That's the problem," she whispered so low that be barely heard it.

Setting his untouched glass on the coffee table, he took hers from her and placed it next to his. Taking her hands in his, he brought her hands to his lips and brushed them across her knuckles. Her body visibly relaxed, but there was still a little tension left that he knew only her coming to terms with his past would release.

"I can't change the past. But I can guarantee I will never be in another movie. And if you want I can sit down and list every movie and what happened in them, though I doubt that would make you feel better."

She shook her head and her body shuttered as if she were trying to hold back her emotions. "It just... The girls at the coffee shop. They all saw you fucking another woman, or women. I didn't ask which. Hell, I wouldn't be shocked if Samantha rents out the Hunter collection just to rub it in my face."

Hunter let out a loud sigh. "I can only imagine how that feels for you." He hooked his index finger under her chin and forced her eyes to meet his. "To be honest... It would tear me apart if I knew men could watch you fucking other men whenever they wanted to."

"And Samantha... She loved rubbing it in, you know?"

"You could always quit and work for me," he suggested with a little chuckle, but at the same time if she was interested he couldn't imagine anything sexier then having the woman he was with at his side during film production.

For the first time since he'd picked her up at the coffee shop she laughed. Leaning forward she gave him a quick kiss. "How much work do you think you'd get done with me on set with you?"

He wiggled his eyebrows at her, causing her to giggle. "Oh, I think it could be *a lot* of fun." He returned her kiss, but his kiss was deeper and more intense. She moaned against his lips, leaning into him and flattening her hands against his chest.

He settled back onto the sofa and pulled her up onto his lap so she was straddling his thighs. She'd changed into a camisole and loose fitting knee length skirt. The skirt hiked up her thighs to her waist as she straddled him giving him a glimpse of her pink satin panties.

The fire within him ignited. He knew he needed to continue talking with her over the porn issue. She needed to be reassured that he wasn't the man in those videos anymore and hadn't been for a long time. She was making him realize that what he was missing in his life was the love and stability of a sweet, caring woman.

A woman like her.

Chapter 8

Nadine tugged at the hem of his snug fitting t-shirt pulling it up over his finely defined muscular abdominals and chest. Lifting his hands to the ceiling, Nadine pulled his shirt up all the way off and tossed it to the floor. Sitting back on him, she traced the contours of his muscle with her fingertips.

"It's no wonder you were so popular in the movies. You're gorgeous Hunter."

He chuckled and he smiled shyly. "Come on now, you'll be kicking the ego you claim I have into overdrive if you keep it up."

Bending over she kissed a trail of butterfly kisses along his collar bone, while tugging at his belt with her eager fingers. "Sometimes, an ego isn't too bad."

He raised a sceptical brow at her. "Really?"

Nadine nodded and sat back on him again, chewing nervously at her lower lip. "Can I ask you something?"

Hunter, reached over and ran a hand through her hair, and watched the dark strands slowly fall from his fingertips. After what felt like an eternity to Nadine, he nodded. "Of course. Anything."

"What *have* you done in those videos?" She wasn't sure if she wanted to know, but it would bother her if she didn't ask.

Hunter shrugged. "What *haven't* I done?"

Nadine clucked her tongue off of the roof of her mouth. "So can we try some stuff?"

"Stuff?" The sexy grin that sent Nadine's heart racing returned and he slipped his hands to her ass, pulling her tighter to his growing dick.

"But, nothing real nasty or anything."

Hunter raised an inquisitive brow at her.

She grinned sheepishly at him, slightly embarrassed to have brought it up. "Well, maybe a *little* kinky."

His hands caressed her ass cheeks, his fingers moving close to her dampening pussy. Closing her eyes, Nadine savoured the feel of his fingers, and moaned softly as he slipped a finger under her panties and stroked the length of her slit. She leaned forward and kissed the side of his neck. "Or we could just do it here on the sofa."

"Hmmmm." Pulling her tight, he stood with her in his arms. "I have an idea."

Nadine yelped in surprise, wrapping her legs around his waist and arms around his neck. "Where are we going?" she murmured nipping at his earlobe.

"Bedroom. Oh, wait until you see what I have in mind."

"Oh yeah?"

"But if you don't want to, then don't be shy to tell me. Or feel obligated to try." Carrying her through the bedroom threshold, Hunter carried her over to the massive four poster king sized bed and laid her onto it, settling himself between her legs.

Nadine moaned, wiggling under him anxious to feel him in her again. She doubted she'd ever have enough of this man, ever. Everything about him felt too good. Physically and emotionally.

"S-s-sooooo. Wh-what do you have in mind?"

Hunter pulled up and braced his body over her with a hand on either side of her head. Their eyes locked and the desire flaring in his eyes sent shivers through her. "I'm thinking we should record it."

Nadine froze under him. "You mean..."

Hunter chuckled. "The disc will go to you. I don't get a copy. It's all yours to do with as you please."

Part of her was scared over the idea. Would her ass look lumpy? Would she look like she was inexperienced? Would it matter if she did since she was the only one to get a copy. On the other hand, the thought of being able to watch it whenever she got horny and Hunter wasn't around did seem appealing. And there was the fact that she'd have a video of him that was for her eyes only. She really liked that. And there was also a certain thrill that came with the idea of being taped.

Hunter frowned. "You know what. I'm sorry, it was an impulsive silly idea. I-"

"Yes!"

Cocking a brow up at her he confirmed, "Yes?"

Nadine nodded. "Let's do it. I like the idea of having a Hunter Robert's original in my video collection."

Laughing, Hunter kissed her quickly on the lips and slid off of her and made his way to his closet. Within minutes he had a camera and tripod set up and pointed towards the bed. A sliver of fear rushed through Nadine, mixing with the passion and excitement as she sat up on her knees and watched him set up the equipment. "Now this isn't going to be the quality of my, ummm," He cleared his throat nervously, "*other* videos. But it's a damned good camera so it'll suit for our purposes."

Was she seriously going to do this? She suddenly became self-conscious. She trusted him. The video was going to be her, for her eyes only if she liked. She wouldn't even need to share it with Hunter. But, it still pulled her out of her comfort zone. How was he able to perform in all those videos? She had no idea.

"Does it get easier?"

Finished fiddling with the camera, Hunter looked up to catch her nervous gaze. "Making videos?"

Nadine nodded.

"Yeah, it does. Between you and me, I was terrified the first time. Came way too fast, was clumsy. It was a mess." He shrugged and gave her a lopsided grin. "I got better."

Nadine couldn't imagine Hunter being clumsy or unsure of himself - with the exception of the incident at the hot tub. The memory brought a grin to her face and her insecurities began to melt away leaving the intense hunger for him.

"We're filming," Hunter advised.

Stepping up to the bed, his back to the camera, blocking the shot of her, Hunter slipped a hand to the nape of her neck and leaned down, claiming her lips with his. The kiss that began as sweet and tender quickly intensified. Hooking her index fingers into the belt loops on his jeans she pulled him closer to the bed - and her.

She sighed softly against his mouth and he took the opportunity to slip his tongue between her lips to explore her mouth. The simmering between her legs ignited to a full fledged inferno of want and need. The video camera was forgotten. All that mattered was him and shedding the pesky clothing that was keeping them separated.

Their tongues continued to frolic, as she finished undoing the front of his jeans and pulled them down over his hips in a single yank. Tearing her mouth from his, Nadine stroked this rock solid cock over his boxer briefs. She was about to pull down the briefs when he stopped her.

"Not yet."

Nadine groaned inwardly. "You say 'no' way too much Hunter."

Chuckling softly, Hunter slid onto the bed and moved behind her. She was about to turn to face him, but he grabbed her upper arms keeping her where she was, on her knees facing the camera straight on. Remembering the camera pointed at them, she realized what he had planned and the self-consciousness crept back into her mind.

"You're beautiful honey," he reassured her, his voice flowing through her like satin and putting her at ease.

Brushing her long silken locks to one side he ran the tip of his finger down the length of her neck from her ear lobe to her shoulder. A shutter rushed through her and she let her head fall to the side and back against his shoulder, allowing his mouth access to the sensitive flesh.

His lips and teeth kissed and nipped at her neck, sending shivers through her. Grabbing the hem of her camisole he slowly peeled the garment up over her stomach. The feel of his hard body against hers along with the sensations flowing through her from his kisses, made her forget that she felt her stomach wasn't perfectly defined and flat. Before Hunter she'd never have dreamed of going outside in a bikini or being videotaped, but Hunter made her feel like that it didn't matter, she was beautiful and desirable as she was.

She lifted her hands above her head as the camisole was pulled up over her moderately sized breasts and off. Reaching behind her, she grabbed his hips and pulled his cock tightly against her ass, bucking back against him.

He growled softly in her ear, pulling the cups of her bra down and palming her breasts. His fingers rolled and pinched her nipples between them, turning them into hard, tightened peaks as she gyrated against him, whimpering softly.

Releasing her breasts, Hunter reached being her and unzipped her skirt. It fell from her hips to puddle at her knees, leaving her in just her bra and panties. Next went the bra. With a flick of the wrist, Hunter had the bra undone and was sliding it down her shoulders.

"Open your eyes," he said. Hooking his index finger under her chin, he tilted her face up to his.

Slowly she opened her eyes and was shocked to see the intensity of his desire flaring up in his dark eyes. Her pussy clenched and the only thing she could think of was her need to have him in her.

"I need you in me," she whispered. Reaching behind her once more, she hooked her thumbs in the waistband of his boxers and tugged them down. His dick pressed up against her ass and a dollop of pre-cum dripped onto her back.

Hunter backed away from her, and she groaned her protest. "Get rid of the panties for me."

Nadine became aware of the camera once more and hesitated momentarily. Taking a deep breath in, she summoned up the courage to stand and finish slipping out of her skirt. Wanting to make her image in the video was sexy as possible she squared her shoulders and thrust her breasts forward. Hooking her thumbs into the waistband of her panties - which were now drenched in her juices - and facing the camera, she slowly peeled them down and let them drop to the floor.

Not hearing Hunter come up behind her, she gasped when his arms wrapped around her waist, and pulled her naked ass back against his dick cupping her mound. While she'd been stripping he'd also removed the remainder of his clothing.

"Get on the bed, on your hands and knees, kneeling diagonal to the camera."

"Okay..." She did as told and waited, her eyes following him as he walked over to the night table and he pulled out a bottle of lube and a... butt plug? She'd never had a butt plug inserted before. Heck, she'd never had anal before. It was slightly intimidating, but her desire overruled her apprehension.

Hunter got onto the bed with her and moved to settle between her legs. He groaned softly, low and feral as he slid two fingers between her dripping wet folds. "We won't be needing the lube."

Hell no. She doubted she'd ever need lube with him since a single touch from him set her body aflame.

He ran two fingers along her slit again, and she moaned, bucking back against his hand. Wanting more, needing more. "Hunter..." she half-moaned, half-sighed, fisting the blanket under her.

He stroked her again, with one hand, while he other rolled her swollen clit between his fingers. Nadine bucked against his hand with more force, her breasts jiggling with the motion. When he stroked her a third time, he lubbed her ass with her juices. His index finger lingered at her anus, pressing against the tight rim of muscle guarding her back entrance.

She pushed backward against his intruding finger, wanting to know how it felt to have her ass invaded. He pressed harder into her ass and she whimpered as his finger pressed into her back entrance to the first knuckle. She cried out, fisting the blanket tighter.

"You've never-"

"No!" She wanted more and moved against his hand.

He continued to stroke her clit, rougher and harder, as he began finger fucking her ass. The sensations were so foreign, but *so* good. The sensations rushing through her was becoming too intense, all thought was lost on her except her rapid ascension to her breaking point.

"I need it now! Please..." She fell to her elbows, her chest against the mattress and her cries of pleasure muffled by the blanket. Closer and closer, until she was there, teetering on the brink.

"Come on honey. Let me feel you let go."

His voice washed over her, so deep and sexy. One final wave of pleasure rushed down her spine and she was finally given her relief. Her stomach clenched as her body let go, a rush of her juices flowing from her to coat his teasing fingers.

"Mmmm, I love the sounds you make when you come," Hunter murmured as he leaned over her and kissed her lower back.

Hunter never gave her a chance to recover. The finger that had been in her ass was immediately replaced by the slender anal plug. And his teasing fingers were replaced with his cock, running back and forth between her puss lips.

Her body came alive a second time yearning for his thick dick. ""Give it to me," she begged, pushing back against him as the head of his cock pressed against her entrance, in an attempt to impale herself.

*****

"Dammit, I can't get enough of you." Hunter groaned as he pressed the head of his cock slowly into her warm, juicy pussy. She groaned under him, her back arching and bottom gyrating back against him, urging him in further.

He loved the sight of her, and could only imagine how stunning she was going to look on video - if he was allowed to view it with her. He planned to be true to his word. It was for her viewing only unless she allowed him the privilege as well.

Everything about her was so alluring. In porn, the sex was so rehearsed to the point it lost most of its arousing qualities for him. She was so raw, so needy. Her lust for him was honest and her desire to please him sincere. For people in their industry the lines between acting and raw genuine pleasure sometimes became blurred. Perhaps that was why sex had lost much of its appeal for him over the years - until Nadine.

Slowly, he slid the remainder of the way into her. Her channel took him in fully begging him to remain there. He groaned softly, caressing her round ass. He wanted to fuck her hard and fast, but held back waiting for the ultimate rush of having her beg him for it instead.

Just when he didn't think he could restrain himself any longer he heard what he'd been waiting for. "*Please* Hunter." The desperation in her voice was like erotic music to his ears. Still fighting to keep hold of his self-control, he began to move within her. Slowly, at first, but as her moans and the need for release intensified so did the force and speed of his thrusts.

Her whimpers and moans combined with his feral groans filled the room as their bodies worked in unison. She screamed out under him, her pussy quivering around his throbbing cock which was greeted with a surge of her juices. Instead of stopping he kept going, not giving her time to recover before forcing her to ascend the summit of her desire once more. Just when he was sure he couldn't hold back a second longer, Hunter pulled out and flipped her over onto her back.

Nadine groaned her displeasure with him for stopping, looking up at him with eyes so full of raw lust that he nearly came then and there. Taking a deep breath in to keep his cock under control, he slid her legs over his shoulders so her ass was suspended in the air and slammed back into her drenched pussy.

Closing her eyes she arched her back and fisted the blanket under her as she moved with him, meeting each of his thrusts. Glancing up, he noticed the camera straight ahead of him that he'd long since forgotten about.

Lifting her just an inch higher so the angle for the camera would be ideal, Hunter continued pounding into her sweet pussy, his balls slapping against her ass. His eyes followed each in and out movement, watching his cock disappear and reappear from within her shaved cunt. It was an intoxicating sight.

Nadine writhed and moaned under him. Hunter's eyes shifted back down to her breasts. Her eyes opened back up and followed his. She began to palm her breasts for him - enticing him - and pinched her nipples between her fingertips.

"Oh God. Oh God, I'm coming!" she cried out as her body tensed under him and her pussy milked his cock as if begging him to join her in her climax.

The sensations were too intense. He'd gone too long without release. With one final thrust into her, burying himself to the hilt, he felt the rush of pure pleasure that ran from the top of his head to the tip of his toes. He shot several bursts of cum deep within her core and as he pulled out another couple of spurts layered her pussy and stomach.

Exhausted, Hunter flopped down on the bed and pulled her into his arms. Though panting hard, she snuggled up against him, while he reached behind her and removed the anal plug. She let out a sigh of relief, laid her head on his chest and draped a leg across his thighs.

"So is that what you called the money shot earlier at the shoot?"

"Huh?" Shaking his mind clear of the after sex cobwebs he raised an inquisitive brow at her, not sure if he had heard correctly.

She ran her index finger along her pussy and stomach and then brought her cum covered finger to her lips. "The money shot."

A burst of laugher erupted from him, so hard that by the time his laughter subsided his stomach ached. "Nah, the real money shot took place inside that amazing pussy of yours. That was just a bonus."

"Mmmmm. Either way it was amazing."

"You know, I don't think I've grown so attached to anyone this quickly in my life Nadine."

She turned in his arms and propped her chin on her arm looking deep into his eyes. "Me too." A soft glow coloured her cheeks as she said it that tugged at his heart. A heart he'd kept well guarded over the years.

"So, am I still cocky and arrogant?"

"Oh, you have *got* to get over that." Nadine giggled, kissing his chest. "Worse than ever, but regardless I'm falling for you."

His heart stopped for a long moment as he gazed into her eyes. She'd just spoken what he was beginning to feel. What had it been four days? Five? Since they went out on their first date. Three months since the first day she served him at the coffee shop and for every day after that he made it his religion to stop there just too see her. It sure as hell wasn't for the foul tasting coffee they served there. It had all been to see her, and capture that five or ten minutes of conversation a night. Yes, he was falling hard for her. Hard, fast, and it was as scary as hell.

"Me too," he whispered kissing her temple and pulling her tighter to him.

Within minutes they were asleep in each others arms, the camera long forgotten, but capturing every moment of them together.

Chapter 9

"I swear I am going to grab that woman by the hair and chuck her out of the drive-thru window Jenny!" Nadine growled as she yanked her headset off and tossed it onto the small table the staff used on their breaks in the back kitchen.

Jenny grinned, not looking up at the fuming Nadine as she continued washing the commercial sized sink full of pots, banking pans and dishes. "You know you can't take anything she says seriously. She enjoys getting under peoples' skin. It's what she's good at."

Nadine crossed her arms over her chest and watched the fifty-something, tough as nails woman, who all the girls regarded as their mentor, friend and substitute mom while at the coffee shop. "It's not just that. I'm twenty-six and I've lived here all my life. I've never been out of New England if you can imagine!"

Jenny's grin deepened. "Then quit. Leave the city. Start a new life."

Nadine laughed at the absurdity of the idea. Where would she go? What would she do? And she had Hunter now. It had been two weeks since their first date and she had no doubt he could *possibly* be the one.

And Samantha couldn't have been more bitter about it. For the past week Samantha had been dropping hints over some of the stuff that was in his videos. She'd even had the nerve to tell some of the customers that Nadine's boyfriend was a porn actor and pornographer. Nadine wasn't embarrassed over what he did, but she did have a big problem feeling like she needed to explain herself to the customers, who - of course - would have a string of questions. That being said she actually preferred the questions to the peculiar looks she got from those who weren't inclined to respond.

Sam simply made things very uncomfortable for her at the coffee shop. *Jealous bitch.*

"So did you watch the video yet?"

Nadine's face burned with her embarrassment at the mention of the video. Aside from her and Hunter, Jenny was the only one who knew about the video. As promised Hunter had handed her the disc that next morning and hadn't mentioned it sense. There were a number of times that she'd considered popping it into the player, but hadn't gotten up the nerve yet.

Nadine shook her head, her face still burning. "Not yet."

Jenny laughed. "Well get on it hun. Maybe you could have a new career."

Nadine groaned as she looked into Jenny's amused eyes. "I doubt that."

"I think you need to get that video, pop it into the player and watch it with that hot piece of ass you're dating."

Oh-my-God. Leave it to Jenny to say something like that. Pulling her shirt up slightly, she pinched her love handle. "I'm not sure I want to see this on television Jenny."

Laughing, Jenny shook her head. "You're a beautiful girl, why do you think Hunter was attracted to you in the first place."

Nadine grinned and shrugged. "I make a good cup of coffee?" she offered.

"No one makes a good cup of coffee here, hun. It's not possible I've tried for almost ten years."

Nadine took a look around the kitchen. Almost ten years working at a coffee shop - the *same* coffee shop. Seemed like an awful long time to her. Hunter joked a couple of times over the past two weeks about her working for him on set. Could she really work with him as part of a porn crew? She just didn't know.

*****

Hearing Hunter's key unlocking the front door of the house sent Nadine's pulse racing as it did every time she saw, or anticipated seeing, him. He had to work late so told her to go back to his place and wait for him if she liked. He'd given her the key a couple of days ago, and insisted she come over anytime day or night, whether he was there or not.

She fingered the disc in her hand nervously. She heard him in the foyer moments before he emerged into the living room where she was sitting waiting for him. She stood as he walked into the room and rushed over to him intent on flinging herself into his arms when she saw the worn, worried expression on his face and came to a halt in front of him.

"What's wrong?" Closing the distance between them she slipped her arms around his neck as he pulled her into a tight embrace. "Tell me," she whispered against his neck.

"We need to talk," he replied, pulling away from her and taking her hand leading her to the sofa.

Talk? They needed to talk? Isn't that what people did just before they broke up? A shiver of anxiety raced through her. She gulped down the lump forming in her throat.

Sitting down, he pulled her into his lap. Hooking his index finger under her chin, he lifted her face and brought his lips down to hers like he'd done dozens of times before. But this time was different. It was evident in his kiss, needy and demanding, that he still wanted her - had to have her even. When their lips parted she was left breathless, and even more worried than before.

She snuggled up against him, taking a deep breath in and allowing the woodsy scent of his cologne sweep over her. "What do you need to talk about?" Reluctantly she looked back up to meet his eyes again.

Hunter sighed and opened his mouth to speak when his eyes shifted and caught sight of the video she'd left on the coffee table. A grin spread across his face and she felt his dick come to life against her bottom. "Is that our..."

Nadine grinned. "Yeah, I thought we could..." she shrugged feeling her face flush.

"Oh, that would make my day." His grin faded and his expression grew more serious. "I might as well just say this and we can move on from there."

Nadine's brow furrowed, but she said nothing.

"I received an offer to buy out an adult modelling agency which includes several high end locations. The income would be phenomenal and the locations and in-house models would drastically cut my filming costs. It's something I should have done years ago, but I love the east coast and just didn't want to leave."

"Leave the east coast?" Nadine echoed, stiffening in his arms. "You're leaving. When? Where?" She couldn't believe it. She finally met a man she could see herself with for a lifetime and he was leaving her?

Seeing her distress, he pulled her tighter. "I want you to come with me Nadine." His eyes pleaded with her to agree and she saw the real man. Vulnerable and raw shine through the layers he'd been hiding behind for what she guessed was years. Could it be that he needed her as much as she needed him?

"But... but, what would I do for money?"

He tilted his head to the side and gave her a look that said, *Don't be stupid Nadine.*

"So move with you to..."

"L.A."

"So move with you to L.A. and work for you? And live with you?"

"Move to L.A and work *with* me. And yes, of course, live with me."

The thought scared her. She'd be leaving her family, her friends. Her crummy job. Well, okay, she could do without the coffee shop job and Samantha. "No more Portland," she said more to herself than to him, her mind spinning the pros and cons.

"We can come back and visit. Portland is only an airline ticket away."

"When?"

"I leave in three days."

Wow. Three days...There is all the packing. My job.

"We can have movers pack up our belongings for us and have them sent to L.A.," he offered as if reading her mind. He looked over at the coffee table and without warning slid her from his lap, grabbed the disc and popped it into the player. "There's something I have to show you."

Nadine frowned. *On the video?*

It began to play and to her surprise he jumped over the sex to stop it at a section where she was sleeping alone in the bed. "It was still running while we slept?"

He gave her a sheepish grin. "Yeah, I forgot about it until the next morning." He sat back down beside her and took her hand. "There's been something I've been scared to tell you."

Hunter, scared of something. It seemed improbable. "Alright."

He pressed the start button on the recorder. Hunter walked back onto the video with his mobile phone to his ear, chatting with someone. "She's incredible mom." Silence on screen aside from her soft snores. "Of course. As soon as you get back from Italy we'll fly to Miami so you can meet her." More silence, and soft snores coming from her, sleeping soundly in bed. "I think so... Yeah, I do. For the first time in my life mom, I can see myself being married and starting a family."

The rest of his conversation was a blur to her as her mind processed the information. She'd always had a small fear in the back of her mind that maybe she was just something new and different for him. That eventually he'd get bored of her soft-spoken nature and inexperience and want someone sexier, more experienced, more exciting.

"I know I'm moving this faster than it should go, but I don't want to lose this opportunity, but if you won't go then I would seriously consider staying here and giving up the business opportunity. You're too important to me Nadine."

For the first time since she watched the video she met his gaze and saw with a clear mind his feelings for her. Something her co-worker Jenny had called her out on earlier that evening. He was truly falling for her as fast and hard as she was for him. Upon that realization there was no way she could answer any differently then she did.

Sitting up on her knees, she swung her leg across his lap, straddling him. "I'd move anywhere if it meant being with you."

The sexy, cocky grin that had become his trademark when he first started showing up at the coffee shop graced his lips and in one swift, fluid motion he flipped her to her back on the sofa, settling himself between her legs. Grabbing the remote on the coffee table he pressed a couple of buttons and restarted the video from the beginning.

Her arousal flared up, as the ridge of his jean clad cock pressed against her groin. She moaned softly, while wrapping her arms around his neck. Turning her head to take a peek at the television screen she grinned mischievously at him. "I don't look too bad in that video. So do I get to be a porn star when we go to L.A?" she teased.

Hunter scowled at her, brushing his lips across hers. "Only for me honey. Only for me."

As he nipped at her lower lip, and then proceeded to deepen their kiss, with the sound of their moans in the background she knew that she was the luckiest girl in the world, because the sexy, dark-haired, porn star that was the center of many woman's fantasies was hers and only hers.

The End

Soft & Hard Erotic Publishing

www.elixaeverett.com

Contact Information

Website: www.elixaeverett.com

Email: terry towers@hotmail.ca

Facebook: Terry Towers

Twitter: TerryTowersXXX

Works By Terry Towers

Available Now - Singles

Frat Party Partner Swap

Under the Officer's Command

Daddy's Special Christmas Gift

All For Daddy (Taboo Edition)

The Marine's Naughty Sister (Taboo Edition)

Little Virgin Sister's Webcam Show (Taboo Edition)

Doing Her For Dad (Taboo Edition)

Deceiving Him (The Billionaires' BDSM Sex Club)

Her Brother, Her Hero

Her 'What if' Guy (Pursued By The Billionaire)

The Inheritance: Anything He Craves

Available Now - Themed Singles

Taken By The Team (Humiliation And Gangbang Fantasies Fulfilled)

Taken By The Marines (Humiliation, Gangbang And Cuckold Fantasies Fulfilled)

The Cop And The Girl From The Coffee Shop

The Politician And The Girl From The Coffee Shop

The Assassin And The Girl From The Coffee Shop

The Bounty Hunter And The Girl From The Coffee Shop

The Firefighter And The Girl From The Coffee Shop

The CEO And The Girl From The Coffee Shop

The Porn Star And The Girl From The Coffee Shop

<u>Available Now - Series</u>

Hitching A Ride

Hitching A Ride 2: To Trust A Con

Conjugal Visits

Conjugal Visits 2: New Beginnings

Sibling Rivalry

Sibling Rivalry 2: Never Say Never

Sibling Rivalry 3: In It Together

Moan For Uncle

Moan For Uncle 2: Keeping It Secret

Moan For Uncle 3: No More Secrets

Moan For Uncle 4: Skeletons In The Closet

Moan For Uncle 5: Love Or Duty

Moan For Uncle 6: To Love And Honour

Available Now - Mirror Editions

(Please note Mirror Editions are mainstream non-PI editions of some of Terry's bestselling taboo works.)

Doing Her For The Boss (Rewrite of Doing Her For Dad)

The Marine's Naughty Sister (Rewrite of The Marine's Naughty Neighbour)

The Virgin's Webcam Show (rewrite of Little Virgin Sister's Webcam Show)

Seducing Blake (Rewrite of All For Daddy)

Now Available - Bundles

The Terry Towers' Taboo Collection Vol. 1

The Terry Towers' Taboo Collection Vol. 2

Naughty But Nice Mirror Edition Collection

The Moan For Uncle Bundle (Books 1-3)

The Sibling Rivalry Bundle (Books 1-3)

German Language Versions

Taken By The Team (Humiliation and Gangbang Fantasies Fulfilled)

Von der Mannschaft Durchgenommen (Erniedrigungs- und Gangbangfantasien erfüllt)

Taken By The Marines (Humiliation, Gangbang & Cuckold Fantasies Fulfilled)

Von den Marines durchgenommen (Erniedrigungs- und Gangbang- & Fremdgehfantasien erfüllt)

The Marine's Naughty Sister

Die unanständige Schwester des Marines

Moan For Uncle

Sehnsucht nach dem Onkel

Hitching A Ride: Sexy Anhalter (Anrüchiges einverständnis erotik)

Sibling Rivalry

Geschwister Rivalität

All For Daddy

Alles für Papa

Italian Language Versions

Taken By The Team (Humiliation and Gangbang Fantasies Fulfilled)

Abusata dal gruppo (Umiliazione e Fantasie di Gangbang Soddisfatte)

Moan For Uncle

Un gemito per lo zio

Her Brother, Her Hero

Suo fratello, il suo eroe

Spanish Language Versions

Taken By The Team (Humiliation and Gangbang Fantasies Fulfilled)

Abusada por el equipo (Humillación y fantasías de sexo realizadas en grupo)

Moan For Uncle

El deseo prohibido

French Language Versions

Taken By The Team (Humiliation and Gangbang Fantasies Fulfilled)

Prise Par L'équipe (Fantasmes Assouvis D'humiliation Et De Viol Collectif)

Coming Soon

Moan For Hubby (Moan For Uncle 7)

The Politician And The Girl From The Coffee Shop 2: All That Glitters

Works By Nikki Nexus

Available Now - Singles

Daddy Says: Ménage Sex Games

Santa's Brothel

The Confessional: The Naughty Nuns Series

The Fire Eater

Taken By The Team (Humiliation And Gangbang Fantasies Fulfilled)

Taken By The Marines (Humiliation, Gangbang And Cuckold Fantasies Fulfilled)

Available Now - Bundles

Naughty But Nice Mirror Edition Collection

Coming Soon

Taken By The Mob (Humiliation And Gangbang Fantasies Fulfilled)

German Language Versions

Daddy Says: Ménage Sex Games

Papa sagt:Jetzt ein flotter Dreier

Works By Adrian Athens

Available Now

The Welding Instructor

Melting Point

Coming Soon

Men For Sale

Works By Elixa Everett

Available Now - Singles

Escort With 1000 Faces

Lust, Love & Luck

I Conjure Thee (Enslaved To The Djinn)

Midnight Encounter - Seduced By A Vampire (Quickie)

Tag, The Vampire's Game

Erotic Flash: A Vampire's Seduction

Children Of The Vampire King (Non-erotic horror)

Available Now - Series

A Night At Club Vampire

A Night At Club Vampire 2: Nigel

Visions Of The Vampire Queen (Book 1 Of The Vampire Queen Series)

Available Now - Bundles

Vampire Whispers - (Bundle of 4 Erotic Vampire Stories)

Coming Soon

Return Of The Vampire Queen (Book 2 Of The Vampire Queen Series)

German Language Versions

Midnight Encounter - Seduced By A Vampire

Mitternächtliche Begegnung: Von einem Vampir verführt

Works By Angelique Ambers

Available Now - Singles

Forced Into Submission (Her Fantasy, His Pleasure)

German Language Versions

Forced Into Submission (Her Fantasy, His Pleasure)

Mit Gewalt unterworfen (Ihre Träume, sein Vergnügen)

Excerpt From

Deceiving Him: The Billionaires' BDSM Sex Club

By

Terry Towers

Available Now

Chapter 1

"Did you get it?" Lexie looked up anxiously from the computer screen where a young brunette woman was strung up and being caned. She watched as her roommate entered their apartment, after her shift at the *Billionaires Club*. Her roommate, Nadine, a beautiful and slender twenty-two year old, black woman worked as a shooter girl at the club.

"What? No *hello*? No, *how was your shift tonight Nadine*? Nothing huh?" Nadine huffed at her childhood friend as she hung her jacket and tiny black handbag in the coat closet by the front door.

"I want you counting the lashes!" the man in the video yelled out.

Laughing, Nadine made her way across the living room and peered over Lexie's shoulder to the video she'd been watching. "I see you've been doing your homework." Nadine watched for a moment as the brunette counted down between lashes.

"8... 7..." the woman called out, wincing - but only slightly - each time the cane made contact with her reddened ass.

"That girl is taking it like a pro. Props to her," Nadine joked, turning away from the screen, suddenly disinterested.

Lexie huffed and exited the video. She had more important things to find out, such as, whether or not Nadine secured a member badge to the club for her. By the smug look in Nadine's expression she would wager it was a yes.

"So, did you get it?"

Nadine reached down the front of her tight red cut-off tank top and produced a small silver badge, about an inch in length and half an inch in width and waved it under Lexie's nose. Lexie eyed the badge, a wide smile forming on her lips. She was finally going to get into the club that could quite possibly give her the news story of a lifetime, and would kick-start her career as a journalist. She was currently a gossip columnist for a small time local gossip paper in San Francisco. But this story could launch her into the big time; it could turn her into a 'real' journalist. Excited, Lexie made a grab for the badge, but Nadine snatched her hand back and quickly backed away.

Nadine wagged her finger at Lexie. "No, no girl. We're going over some ground rules here first before I give you *anything*."

Lexie sighed and rolled her eyes at her friend. "Look, I know. I know. I heard you the first hundred times you stated your terms and conditions."

"Nah, I think we need to discuss them one more time." She flopped onto the thread bare floral patterned sofa, and gave the badge another shake in the air. "This *could* cost me the best paying job I've ever had. If anyone finds out you're not a member and I gave this to you then I will not only lose the best job of my life, but I *could* be facing legal action."

Lexie ranked a hand through her long flaming red curls and sighed. "Even if caught, you know I would never, *ever* give you up."

"It wouldn't be that hard to link us Lex. We grew up in the same town in Nebraska." she waved at their surroundings. "We share an apartment. I think they'd catch on."

"My legal address is still listed in Omaha," Lexie reminded her standing, crossing the room and flopping into an equally worn matching armchair.

Nadine sighed and passed the badge to her. "I'm trusting you. Don't fuck it up."

With a wide grin on her face Lexie accepted the badge and looked down at it. On the silver plate was the engraving T5S in black letters "So what does T5S mean anyhow?"

"Ummm. Well, here's the thing. I just couldn't walk up to my boss and ask him to give me a member badge."

Lexie shrugged. "I suppose not."

"I managed to get lucky and noticed a badge had fallen from a member's clothing and it was lying on the floor. Now if we happen to see a badge and pick it up we're required to turn it in to management. Instead, I tucked it into my bra and kept working. I could be fired for that alone, you know."

Lexie nodded. She doubted she could ever come up with the words to describe the gratitude she felt towards Nadine for sticking her neck out and risking her job to help launch hers. "And I thank you for that. I promise I will make this up to you."

"You're damned right you will," Nadine teased, bending down and unzipping her thigh high stiletto boot.

Lexie looked back down at the T5S and cringed. Something told her she wasn't going to like what it stood for. "So what *does* the T5S mean?"

Nadine sighed and gave her a sympathetic smile. "It means tier five submissive."

Lexie shrugged and stared blankly at her friend. "I have no idea what that means."

Pulling off her first boot she kicked it under the plain wooden coffee table and began unzipping the second one. "Well, to simplify things for their members the club has established a system with those badges. Those labelled with an S or D, submissive or dominant, are ranked one to five."

Glancing down at the badge, Lexie shrugged. "So what does a five do?"

Looking up and meeting her friend's eyes, Nadine grinned and gave her a wink. "You do it all baby."

All? What the fuck does she mean by all?

Nadine continued with her explanation. "You like it as rough as they'll give it to you. Caning, gangbanging, humiliation, electrode stimulation, you like it as hard as they'll give it. Pain is your thang baby."

Lexie blanched, her jaw going slack. "Are you fucking serious?" She'd been watching the videos online that Nadine had directed her to, in order to be prepared for virtually anything and everything she may encounter going on at the club. Doing it *all* was not even close to what she was signing up for.

Nadine groaned, shaking her head. "It's not like you're actually going to *do* any of it. Geez, Lex. Be fuckin' happy I could get you one at all." She reached over to snatch the badge from Lexie's fingers, but Lexie was too fast, jerking the badge out of her reach.

"I am. Thank you Nadine." She stood and gave her friend a quick hug. "I owe you big for this."

Lexie's brow creased when she pulled away and peered over at her friend, noticing the devious look in her expression. "What's that look for?"

Nadine laughed and gave her head a quick shake. "You don't owe me a thing girl. My payment will be getting to see you try and handle yourself in a place like that."

With a huff, Lexie threw herself back in the armchair. "And why would you say that? I've been watching the videos."

Nadine's increased laughter unsettled Lexie slightly. Of course she could handle it; it wasn't as though she was actually going to partake in the... *activities* or anything. She was going solely for the story. Get in, get the story and get out. Easy peasy.

****

"So, here's the deal. I can't guarantee they won't verify membership at the front door even with the badge since you're not a regular, so at 9pm sharp, fifteen minutes from now, the guard patrolling the back loading door is going on his break leaving it unguarded. I'll take my break at the same time and keep him distracted. Got it?" Nadine's voice instructed from the other end of Lexie's mobile phone.

"I got it." Lexie rolled her eyes and then peered at herself in the rear view mirror.

"And for the love of God Lexie. Don't. Get. Caught. Got it."

Lexie huffed in exasperation. "Yes, yes, yes. I got it. Don't worry."

"K - bye."

"Bye." Lexie pressed the release button on her mobile and thrust it into her satin handbag. The minutes felt like hours as she sat in the car and waited for when she could walk down the street and then slip into the back of the club. She was so nervous she was nauseous. Nadine had picked out her outfit which consisted of a strapless red mini dress and black stiletto heeled thigh-high boots. She felt like a damned hooker.

Lexie fingered the diamond solitaire pendant around her neck. The necklace and the matching earrings were on loan from Nadine. Nadine had been given them as a gift from one of the regulars at the club. Talk about perks of the job. *I may look like a hooker, but at least I look like a high priced one*, she mused. She peered at herself in the rear view mirror again, and her anxious emerald green eyes peered back.

After what felt like a lifetime, the clock on the dashboard of the car flashed 8:55. *Showtime,* she muttered to herself. Taking a deep breath to settle her nerves she opened the car door and slid out. Slamming the car door shut and locking it behind her, Lexie made her way down the street towards the club. Just before she came to the front entrance, she veered off into the deserted side alley.

Her heels echoed on the concrete as she quickly made her way down the length of the club towards the back. Just before she reached the corner of the building she stopped and listened. All was silent from behind the building from what she could tell so she continued and rounded the corner.

As suspected it was also empty. Giving the area a quick scan to make sure no one was watching her she confirmed she was indeed alone and hurried to the steel door left slightly ajar. *Thank you Nadine.*

Prying the door open with her finger tips, she slowly and as quietly as possible pulled it open. The beat of techno music greeted her as she peeked in with hesitation. The music wasn't near as loud as you would find at a dance club, but it was loud enough. As promised, the hallway was vacant. Slipping in, she closed the door firmly behind her and turned to her left. Nadine had told her to turn left and then take a right, which would take her to the main room. And that was exactly where she wanted to be.

A rush of excitement accompanied the fear as she squared her shoulders, pulling herself up to her full height of 5'3, luckily her heels gave her an additional six inches and began walking as casually as possible towards the main room.

As she came closer to her destination, the music was accompanied by the sounds of voices. Her excitement raised another notch. She slipped her handbag onto her shoulder making sure the lens of the tiny camera sewn inside was getting a good view of what she was facing. She also had an audio recorder going, but with the music and murmur of voices it would be hard to get anything useful from the audio.

To her relief, she didn't see a soul until she exited the corridor that brought her into the main room of the club. Aside from half dozen cages suspended from the ceiling with naked women trapped in them, at first glance it appeared to be like any other nightclub. Couples chatted at tables, people danced on the dance floor at the center of the room and people hung out at the numerous bars around the room.

"What in the fuck..." Lexie's green eyes widened as her eye glanced over to the far left corner of the room. A small stage was set up featuring a man with three women. The man appeared normal, black pants and a white button down shirt, but the women were dressed in odd looking black leather costumes. Gloves on their hands and boots on their feet which gave the appearance of hooves and they appeared to have long bushy tails. Lexie took a few steps closer.

Are the end of the tails stuck up their...? She grimaced. *Oh God, they are! Damn!*

Lexie watched as the man ordered one of the girls get down on her hands and knees in front of him. She eagerly obliged and he placed a bit gag into her mouth, which was attached to reigns. He "mounted" her with a crop in hand, the reigns in the other. He shouted at her and then brought the crop down at her backside. She cried out, the sound muffled due to the mouth gag. Soon she closed her eyes and began to buck wildly under him.

Double damn!

She noticed Nadine working the room, with tray of shots in hand and quickly made her way over to her. "What's going on over there?" she asked as she approached Nadine, jerking her head in the direction of the display. "That was *not* in any of the videos."

Nadine's dark eyes glared over at her. "What are you doing coming over to talk to me," she hissed at Lexie through clenched teeth as she approached.

"Getting myself a shot," Lexie replied giving her a sweet smile. She selected a shot from the tray and gulped it down. The alcohol burned as it rushed down her throat making her cough and sputter for a moment. It had been literally months since she'd had anything of an alcoholic nature to drink.

"They're called pony girls."

"Pony girls? I don't believe they were part of my homework Nadine." She grabbed a second shot and drank it down. Still burned.

"Yeah, well. Marcel is the pony Master and he's here today to give a performance."

"So who's Marcel? Anyone important?"

Nadine shrugged. "Owns a chain of hotels or something. There's a lot bigger fish here tonight. Saw a couple of actors earlier and some rapper."

Lexie grinned. The crowd of roughly one hundred people in the main room was only a fraction of the people that was in the club at the moment. Nadine had informed her earlier that all members had private suits set up in the building to accommodate their fetish of choice. So most of the members she assumed were occupying themselves elsewhere in the building. She just had to keep her eyes peeled.

She crinkled up her nose as she eyed Marcel and his pony girls. "So he gets off on riding them and slapping their asses with a riding crop?"

Nadine shrugged. "People get off on a lot worse. Check out the water room."

Lexie cast a sideways glance over at her friend and raised a brow. She had a pretty good idea of what went on there and had no desire to check out that room anytime soon. Now finding out *who* was in that room... Oh yeah, that would be useful information.

"Look girl. I gotta go before you get me in shit."

"But..." Taking note of Nadine's anxious expression she nodded. "Okay. Sorry."

Nadine shrugged and leaned into her. "Stay out of trouble and if you get caught..."

"I don't know ya." Lexie finished for her, with a grin.

8131732R00069

Printed in Great Britain
by Amazon.co.uk, Ltd.,
Marston Gate.